The Adventures of
Tiller and Turnbuckle

Adventure One
St. Simons Island

Michael E. Paul

ISBN: 1-4392-4792-7
ISBN-13: 9781439247921

Visit www.booksurge.com to order additional copies.

Acknowledgements

I want to thank the following people for their editing skills and creative ideas:

Brian Goodwin, Betty Ann Howard, Skip Howe, Diane Knight, Margaret Meachum, Patricia Palmer, Judy Rice, Everett Michael Shawen, Tina Thomas, and Michele and Allan Woods.

Thanks to Robert Munsch for his wonderful story, *Love You Forever.*

A special thanks to my mom, Genevieve, and my Georgia Mom, Jean the book lady, for their encouragement, enthusiastic support, and love.

And particular thanks to Kiska the cat and her mom, Pamela Mueller. Their inspiration and direction helped bring Tiller and Turnbuckle to life!

Prologue

"A cat and a dog are the last two animals on earth that I would have expected to be best friends. But then Tiller was no ordinary dog, and Turnbuckle was no ordinary cat," said Grandpa Dachshund to his seven grand puppies all snuggled together in a heap of hounds. The puppies had been named after the parts of a sailboat because of a long tradition of sailing in the family. There was Luff, the littlest of the litter; Rudder, the reliable one who steered clear of danger; Dinghy, the dreamer who wandered away; Cleat, the clever one who knew the ropes; Boom, who always banged his head; Starboard, the stubborn *one who thought he was always right; and Anchor, the anxious one who liked to stay in one place.*

"Cats and dogs can't be friends," said Starboard.

"Sure they can," corrected Cleat. "They just have to get to know each other."

"That's right, Cleat," said Grandpa Dachshund. "Tiller was a dachshund just like you, and he loved adventure. One day, he met a calico cat named Turnbuckle. She not only loved adventure, she loved to play tricks, too. Once Tiller and Turnbuckle got to know each other, they had many adventures together."

"Tell us one, Grandpa, please," said Dinghy.

"Very well. Would you like to hear how they met?" asked Grandpa Dachshund.

"Yes!" yelped the seven puppies at the same time.

But, before Grandpa could begin the story, Dinghy suddenly wiggled free from the heap and ran off to a nearby tree.

"Oh Dinghy, you're always wandering away. Couldn't that wait?" requested Rudder.

"No way," said Dinghy from the tree. "When you gotta go, you gotta go!"

"Oh Dinghy, you say the strangest things," cried Cleat.

Dinghy scampered back to the pile and jumped into the middle, feeling much relieved.

"Ouch, that hurt!" bellowed Boom. "You landed right on my head."

"Dinghy, why can't you just stay in one place?" asked Anchor.

"Okay, Grandpa, I'm ready now. Tell us how they met," said Dinghy.

"Well," said Grandpa Dachshund, "one windy day Tiller was sailing his wooden boat, Dogspeed, down the Chesapeake Bay. Tiller loved to sail. In fact, he was happiest when he was sailing his boat as fast as it could go. Tiller sailed and sailed until he found himself sailing the ocean blue."

Chapter One

Sailing the Ocean Blue

"As long as the wind blows, I'm going to keep sailing," said Tiller to the birds and the sky and the fish and the water. He sailed through the night and through the next day. Even when a terrible storm lashed his little boat with fierce winds and caused a long rip in his sail, he simply took down the sail and continued on with a smaller one saying, "As long as the wind blows, I'm going to keep sailing."

Then, on the third day, the wind stopped as suddenly as it had come. It was almost as if the wind knew the perfect time to stop, for not far off in the distance lay a lovely island. The first thing Tiller noticed was the tall lighthouse, so he steered toward it. A strong current pulled Dogspeed closer and closer to the island and soon Tiller could see gentle waves washing up on white sand dunes. He drifted into a small cove behind the dunes and said to himself, "This is a perfect spot to anchor my boat." He gently turned the boat until her bow faced the wind, and then he...

"Grandpa, what is a bow?" asked Luff.

Boom interrupted, "It's half of a bow-wow." The other puppies laughed.

"Now Boom, stop teasing your brother," corrected Grandpa Dachshund. "Luff, a bow is the front of a boat."

"Does that mean that a wow is the back of a boat?" asked Luff.

The other puppies laughed again. "No, Luff. The back of the boat is the stern."

"Oh. Thank you, Grandpa."

"You're welcome, Luff. Now, where was I...?"

He gently turned the boat until her bow faced the wind, and then he lowered the sail. With skill that only comes from years of experience, Tiller then gathered the sail and tied it tightly around the boom. Next, a few carefully placed paws on the slippery sloop brought him to the bow where he untied the anchor and lifted it from the deck. He eased it over the side, letting the anchor line slowly slip through his paws. As the anchor hit the water, Tiller suddenly felt the anchor line on the deck wrap tightly around one of his back paws.

The next thing he knew, he was being pulled off the deck of his boat into the water. He took a big gulp of air just before the line dragged him under the surface with the anchor. Tiller struggled to free himself, but he was hanging upside down by his back paw, and it was not easy to reach up with his front paw. Tiller's life flashed before his eyes, and, strangely, he thought he smelled bacon-flavored dog biscuits. Just as his breath was about to give out, he felt something tugging at his back paw. The next thing he knew, he was free from the anchor line. With only seconds left before he passed out, he paddled his little legs as hard as he could. When his long snout cleared the water, he sucked air in like a vacuum cleaner.

After Tiller shook the water from his face, he saw a calico cat with big green eyes swimming next to him.

"Are you okay?" she asked.

"Yeah. Thanks for saving my life," said Tiller, coughing up water.

"No problem," she replied. "I just happened to be taking a swim when I saw you fall off your boat."

"Lucky for me," said Tiller. "Let's swim over to the side of my boat. We can climb up the ladder."

With her sharp claws stretched out, the cat gracefully climbed the ladder, for climbing is what cats do. Tiller followed her, although he was not nearly as graceful. "Wow! Nice boat you have here," commented the cat, shaking water everywhere. The fur on her body dried to an orange and black, like a calico sunset on legs, and her head and tail fluffed out as white as snow.

"Thanks. Would you like a tour?"

"Sure."

Tiller led the way down a small ladder into a cozy cabin. The low wooden ceiling was painted white and had strong wood beams to support it. There was a big hatch in the middle of the ceiling and a small round porthole on each side of the cabin to let in light and air. A brass kerosene lantern hanging from the ceiling swayed as Dogspeed rocked gently. Tiller pointed to the right side and said, "This is my little stove where I bake my bacon-flavored dog biscuits. And next to it is my little sink. I use it mostly as a water bowl."

"Is this little bench on the left side where you sleep?" asked the cat, noticing a small blue and yellow quilt covering the bench. Stitched into the center of the quilt was a sailboat that looked like Dogspeed, and it was signed "Mommy" at the bottom.

"No. I usually just take cat naps, I mean dog naps, there. I sleep up in the front of the boat where I can hear the water tapping on her bow. It helps me fall asleep."

"I know what you mean," said the cat. "I can only fall asleep to the sound of the waves crashing on the shore outside my little beach house."

Without warning, the cat raced across the wood floor of the cabin, flew up the ladder, and landed on the deck. Tiller followed her, thinking, "I guess that's the way cats are."

The cat stood, looking up the tall wooden mast, and said, "I bet she sails fast."

"She does. I'd take you for a ride on Dogspeed, but my sail was torn in a storm after I left the Chesapeake Bay."

"The Ches a what?" asked the cat.

"The Chesapeake Bay in Maryland."

"Wow! That's a long way from Georgia."

"Georgia? You mean I've sailed all the way to Georgia?" asked Tiller.

"It would appear so. Hey, after such a long sail, you look like you could use a relaxing swim to East Beach. It's just over there," said the cat, pointing to a long, white line of sand.

"I seem to do better relaxing on my boat than in the water," replied Tiller.

"Oh, there's nothing to it, doggie. Just try to paddle on top of the water instead of under it."

Without warning, the cat jumped; however, as she did, her back paw caught the railing and caused her to perform a perfect flip into the water. Of course, Tiller hadn't seen her paw catch on the railing, so he thought she had flipped on purpose.

"I meant to do that," she said, looking up at Tiller.

"Wow! That was amazing," he said. Tiller decided to do a flip and stepped over the railing. He leaped, he flipped, and he did a perfect...belly flop. A very long belly flop.

"Yaooooow, that hurt!"

"You're funny," said the cat.

"What? I meant to do that," replied Tiller.

The cat just smiled. She was beginning to see that this was no ordinary dog.

Unlike his underwater adventure, this time the cool water felt refreshing to Tiller's long brown body. Paddling next to the cat, he asked, "Isn't it unusual for a cat to be swimming?"

"Oh yes, quite unusual. Cats don't like the water, but when you grow up on an island, you learn to like it."

Tiller was beginning to realize that this was no ordinary cat.

The two touched the sandy bottom and walked out of the water, together. The warm sand felt so good under Tiller's large padded paws. Sand and water flew everywhere as Tiller and the cat shook themselves dry.

The cat extended her black paw to Tiller and said, "Welcome to St. Simons Island. My name is Turnbuckle. What's yours?"

Shaking Turnbuckle's paw, he replied, "My name is Tiller. Nice island you have here."

"Thanks. Say, Tiller, how would you like a tour of the island?"

"Sure. Can we visit the lighthouse? It's the first thing I saw of the island from the ocean."

"You bet. Let's go," said Turnbuckle with playful eyes and a mischievous smile.

Chapter Two

The Sweet Ride to the Lighthouse

Tiller and Turnbuckle ran playfully across the beach and in no time were dashing down Ocean Boulevard toward the lighthouse. Out the corner of her eye, Turnbuckle noticed a large blue pick-up truck approaching them from behind with the words "Sweet Mama's Bakery" printed on the side. "Yes, a shortcut to the lighthouse, plus dessert!" she thought.

"Tiller, follow me!" shouted Turnbuckle. Just as the truck passed, Turnbuckle darted directly behind it and took off after the truck. Tiller did his best to keep up with her. He had a large grin on his face, for chasing large, moving, metal objects is what dogs do.

"I can't believe she chases after trucks, too!" he thought.

"What are we doing?" cried Tiller above the roar of the truck's engine.

"We're taking a shortcut to the lighthouse. By the way, are you hungry?" asked Turnbuckle.

"I'm starving."

"Then get ready to jump."

"Ah, Turnbuckle, jumping isn't really my thing," protested Tiller. "It's not good for my long back."

"No problem," said Turnbuckle. With that, she leaped a perfect leap, for that is also what cats do, and grabbed onto the back of the truck. She stretched her arm down and said, "Grab my paw, Tiller."

"I'm trying!" hollered Tiller, running faster and faster.

"Come on, Tiller. You can do it."

Tiller and Turnbuckle couldn't see the stop sign up ahead. Just as Tiller reached up and grabbed Turnbuckle's paw, the truck stopped. In one swift, cat-like motion, Turnbuckle pulled Tiller right off the ground, and two hairy bodies that looked like sky divers flying sideways went zooming through the truck at thirty miles an hour. For the second time in one day, Tiller's life flashed before his eyes. This time he thought he smelled a ham bone. The only thing that saved them was… the cake.

The large seven-layer cake, lovingly made by Sweet Mama, had said "Happy Birthday Aunt Dee." That was until Tiller and Turnbuckle had both performed "face plants" into the cake, where they remained for a few seconds until the shock wore off. Removing themselves from the cake, they sat up and wiped the icing from their eyes. They looked at each other and burst out laughing. The red icing that had spelled "Birthday" and "Dee" were missing from the cake. Tiller had "Birthday" smeared across his face, and Turnbuckle had "Dee" spread across hers. They laughed even harder when they looked at the cake that now read "Happy Aunt."

The truck had started moving again, and the two sat there licking "Birthday" and "Dee" off their faces.

"Well, shiver me timbers! I don't usually eat dessert, but this is delicious. What is it?" asked Tiller, still licking the letter "y" off his face.

"It's pound cake."

"Funny, it doesn't feel that heavy," said Tiller.

Turnbuckle smiled. "It's one of Sweet Mama's specialties," she said.

"I think I want to marry Sweet Mama."

"Well then you should start eating dessert more often," advised Turnbuckle.

"You're right. How about another piece of that cake?" asked Tiller with a newfound enthusiasm for sugar.

"Good doggie!"

Tiller smiled at his funny new friend, and the two of them sat back and enjoyed the sweet ride.

"So where is this tasty truck taking us, Turnbuckle?" asked Tiller.

"Probably to Sweet Mama's Bakery. From there, it's a short walk to the lighthouse," she replied.

A moment later, Tiller and Turnbuckle jumped off the truck. As they stood watching it turn into Sweet Mama's parking lot, Tiller asked, "What about the cake we destroyed?"

"Let's just hope that somebody has a Happy Aunt somewhere," said Turnbuckle.

They both laughed. "Turnbuckle," said Tiller, "I think this is the beginning of a beautiful friendship."

Chapter Three

Finding Mizzen

A s they continued their walk along Ocean Boulevard, Tiller said, "Turnbuckle, I don't think I have ever seen so many trees and plants living happily together in one place."

Tiller stopped under the shade of several palm trees and looked up at the fronds swaying gently in the warm breeze. Turnbuckle could see by the far away look on Tiller's face that the trees had taken his mind somewhere else. "I just love palm trees," said Tiller. "They bring back very happy memories of sailing the Caribbean Islands with my dad when I was just a puppy."

"Did your dad teach you how to sail?" asked Turnbuckle.

"Yes. And his dad taught him. There's a long tradition of sailing in my family."

With his tail wagging, Tiller twirled around and barked at the beauty surrounding him. "I'm sorry. When I fill up with this much joy, I twirl around and let out a little bark, for that is the way we dogs are."

Turnbuckle smiled. "I understand. When I feel that way, my tail stands up and twitches, and I begin to purr."

They walked a little farther and, suddenly, the sky grew darker and darker, yet the sun was still out. Tiller stopped and looked up. He and Turnbuckle had just walked into a tunnel. But, this tunnel was different. Instead of seeing rock over him, he saw trees, huge trees on both sides of the road whose long, thick, knarled branches had grown together in the middle. "Wow. This is kinda creepy. I've never been in a tree tunnel before," said Tiller. "And what is that stringy gray stuff hanging from the trees?"

"The trees are called live oaks. They're all over the island. That stringy stuff is called Spanish moss. Actually, it's not Spanish, and it's not really moss either," replied Turnbuckle.

Tiller listened with a puzzled look. As they slowly walked through the tunnel, Turnbuckle said, "It was first called Spanish because so much of it was here when the

Spanish humans came. Do you want to hear a legend about how the moss got here?" asked Turnbuckle.

"I don't know. It is going to be scary?"

"Of course not. What could be scary about this island?"

Turnbuckle lay on the sandy soil beside one of the live oaks. "Come on, Tiller, you have to lie down and gaze into the trees while I tell the story."

"Oh man, I can tell this is going to be scary." Tiller lay next to Turnbuckle with his eyes closed.

"One day," she began softly, "an Indian princess died and was buried at the base of a live oak tree."

Tiller shot to his feet, "Not this one!"

"No, silly, not this one."

"Oh. I knew that," Tiller said as he lay back down.

"Anyway," she continued, "an Indian brave, who loved her very much, hung her long black braids on the tree limb to mark her grave. Over time, the braids turned grey and the strands were carried from tree to tree by the wind. To this day all the trees weep for the princess."

Turnbuckle jumped up, startling Tiller. "See, that wasn't scary."

"Okay, but it was kind of sad," replied Tiller.

"Kind of," agreed Turnbuckle, "but this should cheer you up." Without warning, Turnbuckle broke into a run down Ocean Boulevard.

"Here we go again," said Tiller to the live oaks.

"Come on, Tiller. I want you to meet a friend of mine," said Turnbuckle, looking back.

Tiller ran as fast as he could through the tree tunnel and caught up with Turnbuckle a few minutes later. Turnbuckle stopped and said, "Look, Tiller. This is my old school, St. Simons Elementary. Let's go around back to the playground and see if my friend Mizzen is there. You'll like him. He's funny. He should be teaching a class this time of day."

"Okay, as long as he doesn't give me any homework."

Turnbuckle laughed. "Don't worry. It's your first day, so I'm sure that he will go easy on you." They looked for Mizzen, but the playground was deserted.

"So exactly what does this Mizzen look like?" asked Tiller.

"Well, he has white fur and big red eyes, and he's smaller than your ordinary mouse."

"I can't believe you're friends with a mouse!" cried Tiller.

"You'll see that Mizzen is no ordinary mouse. He's kinda old, and he looks after all the other mice on the island, like a grandfather would. He's also the pet mouse at St. Simons Elementary School. The human kids love him. In the summer, they turn him loose, and he teaches the mice on the island everything that the kids have taught him during the school year. Most of our mice know how to read and write," said Turnbuckle proudly.

Tiller just shook his head in amazement.

"I wonder where he could be?" asked Turnbuckle.

"I guess Mizzen is missin'," teased Tiller.

Suddenly, from behind Tiller, a voice with an English accent boomed, "Hello there!"

The loud voice frightened Tiller so much that he shot straight up into the air. He didn't remember leaving the ground, but he did remember hitting his head on the hard tree limb just above him. After he stood and rubbed the top of his head, he looked around to see where the voice had come from.

"Down here," said Mizzen.

Tiller looked down and was amazed to see a little furry rodent sitting up, waving to him.

"Sorry I frightened you. Do mind your head next time, young fellow," advised Mizzen.

Turnbuckle said, "Tiller, let me introduce you to Mizzen."

"Awfully nice to make your acquaintance," said Mizzen, holding out a small, gnarled, pink paw with sharp little claws.

"The pleasure is mine, I think," said Tiller, shaking as much of Mizzen's little paw as he could grab. "That's quite a large voice for such a tiny fellow."

"I get it from my grandfather. He lived in a tall bell tower next to a building called Parliament in London,

England. The bell is called Big Ben, and when it chimes, it is very loud. So, my grandfather, and all the other mice living in the tower, had to talk loudly to be heard over the bell."

Turnbuckle interrupted, "Tiller just arrived here on a sailboat. I'm taking him on a tour of the island."

"Splendid, splendid," said Mizzen. "I do hope you enjoy...watch it, watch it!" he suddenly bellowed, looking over Tiller's shoulder.

Tiller quickly turned to see what Mizzen had seen.

"It's nothing," said Turnbuckle quietly to Tiller. "The older Mizzen gets, the more imaginary creatures he sees trying to move his cheese."

Mizzen hit the side of his head with his pink paw and said, "They're gone. Now, where was I? Oh yes, I do hope you enjoy your stay here on our beautiful island."

"Thank you, Mizzen, I'm sure that I will," replied Tiller.

"Well, I have to scurry off. I think I saw the cheese truck go by a little earlier," said Mizzen.

"Tiller, I'll meet you up on the road in a few minutes. There's something that I want to talk to Mizzen about before he leaves," said Turnbuckle.

Tiller walked up to the road and was joined there a few minutes later by Turnbuckle.

"So, what did you say to Mizzen?" asked Tiller.

"Oh, it was nothing. I'll tell you about it later. Last one to the lighthouse is a rotten egg."

Tiller and Turnbuckle didn't notice the storm clouds gathering over the lighthouse.

Chapter Four

Footsteps in the Lighthouse

Tiller was gaining on Turnbuckle. It felt good to run after several days of just sitting in the cockpit steering his sailboat. Of course, Tiller loved to feel the wind in his face whether sailing or running. What he didn't expect was to feel rain in his face. The wind had begun to pick up, and the air around him quickly turned cooler. His long snout sensed the familiar smell of an approaching thunderstorm. Dark angry clouds rolled overhead as Tiller sprinted the remaining few yards to the lighthouse. Turnbuckle was standing in the doorway when Tiller came to a screeching stop just outside. Using his paws to shield his eyes from the rain, he looked up at the towering wall of the lighthouse and shook his head.

Tiller stepped inside the doorway and caught his breath, "You're one fast feline, Turnbuckle."

"Thanks. And I think you must be the fastest hotdog on four feet."

"Looks like we got here just in time," said Tiller.

"I'll say. But don't worry, these storms don't last long on St. Simons. They blow in and out again pretty fast."

Tiller's nose twitched at the musty smell inside the lighthouse. The brick walls were painted white and a spiral staircase with black metal steps wound around and around, disappearing high over their heads.

"This lighthouse sure looks a lot taller when you're standing next to it," said Tiller. "How many steps does it have?"

"One hundred twenty-nine," said Turnbuckle.

"Wow! That's a lot of steps for a guy with short legs!"

"Not for super doggie and super kitty," replied Turnbuckle. With that, Turnbuckle sprinted through the open door of the lighthouse, shot up the stairs, and disappeared around the bend. Tiller took off after her. It turned out that his short legs helped him keep his balance as he climbed up and up and around and around the spiral steps.

Suddenly, the stairway grew darker as the storm clouds rolled over the lighthouse. Tiller stopped. He stood, surrounded by silence. "Okay, this is getting creepy," he said, looking up the black stairway.

Tiller continued walking, ever so slowly. He tiptoed up one step, then another, then…

"Ahhh!" yelled Tiller. Turnbuckle had jumped out at him as he reached the first landing.

She laughed and said, "You are an easy scare."

"Yes, I am!" he exclaimed. "And I see you like to play tricks."

"Yep. This is going to be fun," she said with a giggle.

But Turnbuckle's giggle was drowned out by a tremendous crack of thunder. At the same instant, lightning flashed through a small window next to them. The light bulb on the landing flickered, sizzled, and went out. Turnbuckle stood in the darkness and Tiller lay as flat on the floor as he could without actually being the floor. His shaking paws covered his ears, and his tail was wrapped between his legs. They both remained still, the only sound coming from the wind howling outside.

It didn't take long for their eyes to adjust to the dark. That's when Turnbuckle heard it. "Hey, did you hear that?"

Tiller meant to say, "What?" But, when he opened his mouth, nothing came out.

"Listen," she whispered.

Tiller lifted his head toward the steps and put his large, floppy, radar-like ears to work.

When he finally spoke, he looked at Turnbuckle and said, "What could be scary about this island?"

Then he heard it, too. "Wait a minute. I really do hear something," he said.

"What is it?" asked Turnbuckle.

"It sounds like screaming!"

"Yes, now I hear it," said Turnbuckle.

The high-pitched screaming grew louder and louder, echoing down the steps of the lighthouse.

"Hey, Turnbuckle, are there ghosts in this lighthouse?"

Turnbuckle shook her head up and down.

"I was afraid of that," said Tiller.

"You see, the lighthouse has always been haunted by footsteps," said Turnbuckle.

"Footsteps?"

"Yep. Footsteps can be heard going up and down the spiral staircase. Legend has it that the footsteps belong to a lighthouse keeper who was murdered by his assistant. The keeper comes back to make sure the light is operating properly. He's really quite harmless."

"Do those footsteps also scream?" asked Tiller.

"Well, not usually," answered Turnbuckle.

"That's it. I'm out of here," said Tiller. But, before he could move, the source of the screaming was upon them. Tiller let out a horrible howl, and Turnbuckle puffed up and let out a horrific hiss. Surely that would turn any ghost around in his tracks. It didn't! The screaming continued just as another flash of lightning lit up the landing enough for Tiller and Turnbuckle to see three human children, a mom, and a dad, who didn't look like ghosts at all, run past them on the landing, sprint down the steps, and disappear around the bend. The screaming quickly faded, and Tiller and Turnbuckle realized that they had let their imaginations get the better of them.

"I can't believe that we thought they were ghosts," said a relieved Tiller.

"I can't believe those humans let a little thunder and lightning scare them," said Turnbuckle.

"Yeah, it's a good thing cats and dogs don't scare so easily," said Tiller.

That mischievous smile spread across Turnbuckle's face, and she shot up the stairs and disappeared around the bend.

"Great, here we go again," Tiller said to the lighthouse.

As Tiller neared the top of the lighthouse, he stopped to listen for Turnbuckle. He wasn't going to let her scare him again! "Turnbuckle, I know you're there." He continued cautiously, his heart pounding louder with each step.

"Surely Turnbuckle can hear my heart beating," he thought as he rounded the last few steps at the top. A huge, black steel door that led to a small round room was open, and Tiller slowly stepped in. He stood in the darkness.

There was a quick flash of light and then the room returned to darkness. At first, Tiller thought it was lightning,
but when the flash came again, he realized it had come
from the great light sending its warning to sailors at sea.
Turnbuckle was standing, still as stone, hair puffed out,
tail straight in the air. Tiller knew something was wrong,
for Turnbuckle did not scare easily. That's when he saw it.
The shadowy figure of a man was floating a few feet off the
floor, checking the light to make sure it was operating cor-
rectly. Tiller thought that it must be his imagination again.
"Please tell me that that's not a..." whispered Tiller.

"I'm afraid it is. Just stand very still and maybe it
won't notice us."

Tiller didn't move a muscle. A moment later the shadowy figure turned and glided past, never taking notice of
them. It seemed to lose its shape as it descended the steps.
The sound of its footsteps echoing off the stairs slowly
faded below them, and Tiller and Turnbuckle found
themselves alone in the silence of the lighthouse, unable
to move or speak. They waited several minutes, listening
for the sound of more footsteps, but none came.

"Now we know why that family was screaming," said
Turnbuckle.

"You did say he was harmless, right?" asked Tiller.

"That's what they say."

Hoping they had nothing to fear from the ghost,
Tiller and Turnbuckle relaxed. The little round room
suddenly filled with light from outside, for the storm had

stopped as suddenly as it had come. As the sky cleared, Turnbuckle's hair and tail slowly returned to normal and Tiller's tail came out from under his legs for the first time since the lights went out.

They stepped out through a small door onto a black metal porch that wound around the outside of the lighthouse and were treated to a most spectacular rainbow out over the ocean. Tiller's tail wagged, and he twirled around and let out a little bark. Turnbuckle's tail twitched and she began to purr for joy at the sight of the storm's reward. They had walked most of the way around the porch, enjoying the view of St. Simons Island, when Turnbuckle stopped and pointed.

"Look, Tiller, way over there is East Beach. That's where your boat is anchored," she said.

Tiller squinted to see his boat. "Turnbuckle, I can't see Dogspeed," he said in a concerned voice. Tiller had excellent vision, and so did Turnbuckle, for that is the way cats and dogs are.

"I hate to say this, Tiller, but neither can I. We'd better get back to East Beach. Let's fly out of here like Mooney's goose," she replied.

Turnbuckle disappeared down the stairs. Tiller followed, scrambling around and around the spiral staircase. He was running so fast that his backside kept passing his front side.

Once he reached the bottom, Tiller tumbled out the door and rolled across the lawn. He looked up at

Turnbuckle and said, "By the way, what is Mooney's goose?"

Turnbuckle giggled. "Oh I don't know," she replied, "it's just something my grandmother used to say."

As luck would have it, Sweet Mama's delivery truck was passing by in the direction of East Beach. Side by side, Tiller and Turnbuckle leaped flawlessly into the back of the truck, leaving the sweet cargo undamaged. Several minutes and desserts later, they hopped down off the truck onto Ocean Boulevard and sprinted the rest of the way to the beach.

"Say, Tiller, you're getting pretty good at this jumping up and hopping down thing," said Turnbuckle as they ran side by side.

"Well, I've never had this much practice before."

"Stick with me, sailor," she said.

Once they reached the beach, their suspicions were confirmed. Dogspeed was indeed gone!

Chapter Five

One Strange Gang of Feathers

Tiller and Turnbuckle stared at each other for a moment. Turnbuckle broke the silence.

"Does Dogspeed often disappear like this?"

"Not usually. If the anchor pulls loose from the bottom, the boat might drift a little, but it usually resets itself somewhere nearby."

"Then I think we're going to need some help," she said.

"Help?"

"Yep. This sounds like the work of the Parrot Gang,"

"The Parrot Gang?" he replied.

"Yep. They're pirates,"

"I thought you said they were parrots?"

"They are."

"Well, are they parrots or pirates?" asked Tiller.

"Yes," replied Turnbuckle.

"Yes, they're parrots or yes they're pirates?" asked Tiller impatiently.

"Yes, they're parrot pirates," said Turnbuckle teasingly. "They're the Parrot Pirate Gang."

"Wait a minute," replied Tiller. "Are you saying that the pirates are parrots?"

"No, I'm saying that the parrots are pirates."

"Oh boy, that really clears it up. So, who is the head parrot?" asked Tiller.

"Oh, the head of the Parrot Pirate Gang isn't a parrot," said Turnbuckle.

"He's not a parrot?" asked Tiller.

"That's right."

"But he is a pirate."

"Of course."

"Well, if he's not a parrot, then what is he?" asked Tiller.

"He's a sparrow."

"A sparrow?"

"That's right. He's called Skipper the Sparrow."

"You're telling me that the head of a gang of parrot pirates is a sparrow?"

"Yep."

"Well, shiver me timbers, matey. That sounds like one strange gang of feathers," said Tiller.

"You don't know how right you are. What do you say we find us a flock of pirates? I think they may have taken your boat to their hideout," said Turnbuckle.

"Is it far from here?" asked Tiller.

"Not far. If we get started now, we can be there in no time."

"What about the help?" asked Tiller.

"Have no fear, long doggie, help is near."

Turnbuckle took off down Ocean Boulevard and, once again, Tiller took off after her.

"Where are we headed this time?" asked Tiller, catching up with Turnbuckle.

"First, we'll look for Mizzen. After he eats his cheese, he usually has dessert at Sweet Mama's. Then we'll stop by my house and grab my brother and sister. My friend, Keel, should be at a restaurant in the village where she helps out the humans. Although, I think she just hangs out there for the treats," replied Turnbuckle.

The two laughed and skipped down Ocean Boulevard. In the middle of a skip, Tiller suddenly thought of a very important question. "Turnbuckle, what do these parrot pirates look like?"

"Well, they're about two feet tall with long tail feathers, and they're so colorful, they look like flying rainbows. Don't let their pretty colors fool you because they have large hooked beaks that…well, just don't get near their beaks."

"How many of these parrots are there?"

"Nobody knows for sure, but the most dangerous ones we know of are Skipper the Sparrow, Pearl, and Black Beak. Pearl is from Jamaica, and you can tell who he is from his accent. Whatever you do, don't stare at the red feathers sticking straight up out of his head. The last doggie who did that disappeared. Rumor has it he became dinner for an alligator. Then there's Black Beak. You'll recognize him by the black patch he wears over his left eye and by his huge, hooked black beak with pieces of it missing. Do not ask him about the missing pieces. Of course, Skipper the Sparrow is the worst of them all. He is smaller than the parrots, but don't let his size fool you. He's four inches of pure meanness. His gray feathers stick out in every direction, and he has big black eyes and wears a small gold ring through his sharp little beak. Oh, and he carries a sharp dagger with a silver handle that he likes to use on tourists."

Tiller's forehead wrinkled with worry. "I should just find a new sailboat… and maybe a new island."

"Don't worry, my little salty dog, those pesky parrots are no match for the fearsome furry friends."

Their walk came to an end when they met up with Mizzen who was just strolling out of Sweet Mama's with powdered sugar stuck to his face. After explaining their situation to Mizzen, he was more than glad to help, especially since it included a stop at a restaurant. Next, it was on to Turnbuckle's house. Knowing that Mizzen could never keep up with the speedy duo, Tiller offered him a ride on his back. As usual, Turnbuckle had already sprinted away.

"Hold on, Mizzen," said Tiller. Mizzen dug his claws in tight and held on for dear life as Tiller raced to catch Turnbuckle.

"My, she is fast," said Mizzen.

"You're telling me; I think I lost her."

Chapter Six

The Warning

Suddenly, Mizzen heard something in the azalea bushes next to the road. "Tiller, stop."

"What is it?" asked Tiller.

"I think I heard a noise over there in the bushes."

"Oh no. I hope it's not another ghost," said Tiller.

"Psst. Over here, you two," whispered a familiar voice.

Tiller and Mizzen cautiously walked over to the bushes.

"Quick. Get in here." Tiller and Mizzen recognized Turnbuckle's voice and ducked into the bushes.

"What's going on?" asked Tiller.

"I spotted two parrot pirates up ahead sitting in a palm tree."

"Great," said Tiller. "Let's go grab them."

"Not so fast. We could be walking into a trap. They would love to get their hands on you," said Turnbuckle.

"They already have my boat," said Tiller. "Why would they want me?"

Mizzen said, "Well, because now that they have another boat for their pirate fleet, they will need more crew. They always take tourists for their crew. Do you know what it means to be shanghaied?"

"Shang who'd?" replied Tiller.

"It's pronounced shang hide, like hide-n-seek," said Mizzen. "When someone is Shanghaied, they are kidnapped, taken by force to do back-breaking work on a ship. That's how my grandfather ended up here on St. Simons Island. He was shanghaied on a cargo ship laden with barrels of bangers from England. As it turned out, Grandfather feasted on the bangers every night, and by the end of the trip, he looked more like a dachshund than a mouse."

"I'm sorry to hear that your grandfather was shang-fried," replied Tiller.

Mizzen just shook his head.

Turnbuckle said, "Tiller, we can't let the parrot pirates see you going to my house or my family could be in danger. Do you remember how to get to my old school?"

"Sure."

"Great. Mizzen and I will distract the parrot pirates while you run and hide around the back of the school. We'll meet you there. Give Mizzen and me a ten second head start."

Mizzen and Turnbuckle walked calmly toward the parrot pirates. Ten seconds later, Tiller ran and never looked back. Now all he had to do was find the school, but the farther he ran, the more the streets started to look the same. "The last thing I need is to get lost," Tiller thought.

Suddenly, he heard the squawking of birds overhead. Without looking up, he darted off the road into a dense grove of palmetto palm trees for cover. The squawking continued, and Tiller expected to be carried off at any moment in the grip of sharp talons when he spotted a wooden footbridge over a tiny stream. He ducked under the bridge, covered his head with his paws, and waited. "How did the parrot pirates find me?" thought Tiller. The squawking stopped and Tiller relaxed. "Boy, that was a close call," he whispered.

Tiller started to get up when he heard wings flapping and a plunk, plunk on the bridge. He froze. The two birds sat just inches over his head.

"Did you see where he went?" asked one of the birds.

"No. I lost him. I was looking the other way," responded the other bird.

"How many times have I told you to look forward when you're flying. Come on, let's get out of here. He's probably just ahead of us," said the first bird.

As the two birds flew off, Tiller heard one of them say, "I hope we can catch that dog to give him Turnbuckle's warning."

"Turnbuckle's warning?" asked Tiller out loud.

He scrambled out from under the bridge and could see that the two birds were not parrot pirates but seagulls. "Come back, please. Come back," he yelled. Tiller could only stand and watch, for they had flown too far to hear his plea.

"Great," said Tiller to the empty woods. "I'm lost, and I don't know what Turnbuckle is trying to warn me about. I guess I'll just have to keep going until I find the school. After all, a sailor never gives up."

Tiller's good sense of direction had never failed him before, and, upon noticing a narrow path leading from the other side of the bridge, he decided to cross over and follow it. He walked and walked. The air became cooler and the sky darker as the palm trees and ferns became thicker and thicker. "What could be scary about this island? What could be scary about this island?" Tiller repeated over and over to calm himself.

Then, the path disappeared. Tiller had to crawl through a dense forest of ferns. As he pushed the large fan shaped leaves out of his face, they kept smacking him on his behind. "This doesn't look good," thought Tiller.

Just when he thought about turning around, he saw a clearing ahead. This lifted his spirits, so he pressed on. He crawled faster and faster until he stood in the open with the sun on his face and the forest of ferns behind him. "Yes. I did it," he said to the sky. "Now all I have to do is…is…cross over this endless, grassy, muddy, swampy, saltwater marsh that's blocking my way in every direction," he yelled. "How could my good sense of direction lead me absolutely nowhere?" cried Tiller to the muddy marsh.

"Oh, I wouldn't say that," came a deep voice from the marsh that rattled the grass and made Tiller's hair stand on end.

Tiller stared into the marsh as the tall golden blades of grass parted. Whoever, or whatever, had just spoken was about to get a whole lot closer. He slowly backed up until a fern leaf struck him in the tail. His yelp echoed out over the marsh. Two big, bulging eyes and a long green snout slithered forward out of the dark, churning water right toward Tiller.

"I'd say it was a good thing that your good sense of direction led you to me," said the creature as he slowly crawled closer. "Permit me to introduce myself. The name is Gunwale, Gunwale the Gator. I have never before had the pleasure of meeting such a long dog here in my marsh. Of course, other smaller, less… how shall I say…filling dogs have wandered this way."

"Well, Mr. Gunwale, sir, it's been awfully nice meeting you, but I don't want to impose, so I'll just be on my way," said Tiller, backing into the forest of ferns.

"Wait!" shouted Gunwale. "I don't mind swallowing, I mean… showing you the way. Here, hop in." Gunwale opened his slimy green jaws wide and lunged at Tiller.

"Ahhh," yelled a startled Starboard suddenly. The other six puppies started yelling, too. Dinghy got so scared that he wet himself.

"Boys, boys, settle down," said Grandpa. "Starboard, what on earth scared you so?"

"Something touched my tail, and I thought the alligator was going to eat me."

"That wasn't an alligator. I was just stretching my paw," said Cleat. "Don't worry, Starboard, I'll keep an eye out for any dog-eating creatures." The six puppies laughed.

"Now boys, don't laugh at your brother. You were all just as scared," said Grandpa with a smile on his face. Grandpa knew

that the puppies loved scary stories, so it gave him pleasure when he scared them. "Now, where was I..." said Grandpa in a scary voice. His seven grand puppies snuggled closer together.

Gunwale opened his slimy green jaws wide and lunged at Tiller.

Tiller had only enough time to shut his eyes as he waited for the gator's gaping jaws to snap closed around him.

Suddenly, he heard the flapping of wings and a plunk, plunk. Tiller felt a mighty rush of wind as the jaws of the gator snapped shut just inches from his face. When he opened his eyes, he saw two birds each perched on one of Gunwale's bulging eyelids. Their claws tightened around the gator's angry eyes and the creature twisted his large head back and forth hoping to shake the birds loose.

"Take that you big green bully," said one of the birds, while pecking the gator's scaly neck.

"Why don't you pick on someone your own size?" cried the other bird that was facing the other way.

"Hey, I was just joking," cried Gunwale. "Let go. That really hurts."

"Oh yeah," said the first bird, "the last time you joked, a small dog disappeared."

"Come on, you guys," said the gator. "A guy has to eat."

"Okay, that's it, you gopher-gutting, grimy gator," said the first bird. "We'd better not see your ugly face around here again. And, if anything else with hair on it disappears, we'll be back!"

"Yeah, and next time the eye surgery is going to be messy," promised the second bird.

The birds squeezed harder and the creature retreated into the water to release his pain. The birds let go just as Gunwale disappeared into the depths of the marsh.

As Tiller inspected his body to make sure that he still had all of his parts, the two seagulls landed next to him. One of the gulls had a white body with gray wings and a black head. His name was Stem. The other had a white body with gray wings and a black tail. His name was Stern. Stem and Stern were good friends, even though they were opposites in many ways.

"Hello, Tiller. My name is Stem, and this is my friend Stern."

Stern, who was facing backwards, said, "Boy that sure was a…"

"Stern!" yelled Stem.

"What?"

"Turn around and face forward when you're talking."

"Oh. Sorry. I'm so used to facing backwards. Where was I? Oh yes. Boy that sure was a close call. Are you okay?"

"I think so," replied Tiller.

Stern continued, "Before it's too late, Turnbuckle has a warning for you. She said that whatever happens, do not, I repeat, do not cross over the wooden footbridge, and do not follow the path into the forest of ferns, and do not continue to the edge of the marsh or you will come face to face with the man-eating, animal-eating, anything-that-falls-into-the-marsh-eating gator named Gunwale."

Stem and Tiller stood, silently, looking at Stern.

"What?" asked Stern.

"Stern," said Stem, "It's over! We arrived too late. Tiller doesn't need the warning."

"Oh."

Stem looked skyward and said, "Give me strength, oh Great Gull."

Stem continued, "Tiller, when you didn't show up at the school, Turnbuckle thought that you got lost, so she sent us to give you a warning and to show you the way back to the school. Sorry we were late. We always arrive late because my friend here likes to look backwards when he flies, and it causes him to go off in the wrong direction."

Stern said, "Hey, my friend, here's a new idea. Maybe you are the one flying off in the wrong direction. And, let me see, did we get here in time to save Tiller's life?" The whole time Stern was talking, he was slowly turning around backwards without realizing it.

"Yes, Stern, we did," said Stem, "but if we had arrived a second later, our friend here would have been gator gourmet!"

"Ooh. Gator Gourmet. What a great name for a restaurant. We could open one on the island and..."

"Stern, stop!" yelled Stem.

"Sorry."

"Anyway, Tiller," Stem continued, "I don't think Gunwale will be bothering you anymore. He doesn't bully anyone under our protection because every time he does, his eyesight gets worse."

"I just want to thank you both for saving my life," said Tiller. "This was a bit more of an adventure than I had in mind when I sailed here."

"Don't mention it. Any friend of Turnbuckle's is a friend of ours," said Stem.

"We know Turnbuckle well," said Stern. "If you hang around her long enough, you're going to have plenty of adventures."

"Speaking of Turnbuckle, we'd better get you to the school. She and Mizzen are there waiting for you," said Stem. "We'll fly just over the tree tops so you can follow us. Hopefully, we won't have too many adventures on the way back."

Luckily for Tiller, there were no adventures on the trip to the school, but it took a little longer than it should have because Stern kept flying off in the opposite direction. Tiller learned just to follow Stem. Eventually they were reunited with Turnbuckle and Mizzen. Stem and Stern waved goodbye as they flew off in opposite directions. Stem flew over the front of the playground, and Stern flew over the back. Of course, Stern was looking backwards as he waved, and he plowed right into a palm tree. After peeling himself from the tree and leaving a feathery outline of a seagull in the bark, he shook himself off and staggered back into the sky.

"I owe my life to those two gulls," said Tiller.

"Actually, only one of them is a gull. The other is a buoy," said Turnbuckle teasingly.

Tiller chuckled. "I sure did miss your sense of humor while I was gone, Turnbuckle."

"Very punny, my nautical friends, but we should be on our way to your house, Turnbuckle," said Mizzen.

"But what about the parrot pirates?" asked Tiller.

Mizzen and Turnbuckle looked at each other and smiled. "Don't worry," said Turnbuckle, "we told them that a tourist seemed to be lost on the other side of the island, and they flew off to find him. That should keep them busy long enough for us to round up the rest of our help."

Suddenly, Turnbuckle took off running in the direction of her house. "Come on you two, it's not far."

"Here we go again, Mizzen," said Tiller. Hop on!"

Chapter Seven

Gathering Help

After a fast and bumpy ride, Mizzen jumped down off Tiller's back, wobbled back and forth for a moment, and then regained his balance. "I know this place," he said. "It is the lovely Beachview Apartments, the seaside home of my fabulous feline friend, Turnbuckle, and her equally fabulous family."

"Thanks, Mizzen," said Turnbuckle.

"Does he always talk like that?" Tiller asked Turnbuckle.

"Always."

The three of them walked into the house.

"Is that you, Turnbuckle?" her mom called from the kitchen. Her soft voice had a soothing southern sound to it.

"Yes, Mom."

Turnbuckle's mom walked into the living room. She was orange and white on top and black on the bottom. She wore a black spot on the top of her head. "Well, hello, Mizzen. And who is this?" she asked.

"This is my new friend, Tiller. He just sailed here all the way from the Chesa, the Chesa,"

"Chesapeake?" asked her mom.

"That's it, the Chesapeake Bay," said Turnbuckle. "I was giving Tiller a tour of the island when we noticed, from the lighthouse, that his boat was gone. We think it might be the work of the Parrot Pirate Gang so we came to ask the two hairballs for their help."

"They're playing on the porch. While you're talking to them, I'll get y'all some sweet tea," said Turnbuckle's mom.

On the screened-in porch, Turnbuckle was attacked by two kittens. The three of them rolled around on the floor until they looked like one big calico hairball. Turnbuckle, after managing to free herself, asked, "What have you two little devils been doing?"

"We were chasing fiddler crabs down by the rocks," they replied.

"Don't let Mom catch you playing down on those rocks," replied Turnbuckle.

"Please don't tell Mom," they pleaded. "Please."

"I won't if you promise to help my new friend, Tiller," replied Turnbuckle. The two had not noticed Tiller because they had been so busy playing with Turnbuckle. At the sight of the strange, long dog the two frightened kittens shot straight up into the air like two hairy rockets. They landed with their hair standing straight out and their claws ready to attack.

"Tiller," said Turnbuckle, "meet my brother, Baggiewrinkle, and my sister, Alee."

The two young cats were the same size, small on the outside and all grown up on the inside. Baggiewrinkle was white on the bottom and black and orange on the top. A black spot sat on the tip of his nose. Alee was orange on the bottom and black and white on the top. A black spot rested on the tip of her tail.

"Relax, you two, Tiller is friendly. He won't bite you," said Turnbuckle. "Sit down while I explain his problem."

Baggiewrinkle hopped up on his favorite little red chair, picked up a bowl of soggy Fruit Loops, and started eating. Alee sat next to him in her yellow chair and held the book she was reading close to her for comfort. Turnbuckle explained Tiller's problem. Immediately, Baggiewrinkle and Alee jumped off their chairs and stood next to Mizzen.

"Well, what are we waiting for? Let's go catch us some bad birds," said Baggiewrinkle. "We'll teach them the proper way to treat a friend."

"Yeah, we'll get justice for Tiller," said Alee.

Mizzen led Baggiewrinkle and Alee in a chant. "Justice, justice, justice!"

"Well, it sounds like y'all are fixin' to find you some parrot pirates," said Mom, walking onto the porch with a pitcher of sweet tea. "Y'all have a big drink of sweet tea before you go."

After sipping the sweet tea, the five furry friends said goodbye to Mom and headed toward the village to pick up Keel.

Chapter Eight

A Walk to the Village

They could have walked to the village along the road, but Turnbuckle preferred the beach, and it just happened to be a shortcut to the village. The tide was out, revealing a wide ribbon of hard gray sand that would be easy to walk on. It was the perfect time to look for shells and sand dollars. Turnbuckle especially loved digging up sand dollars.

As they began their walk, Tiller scanned the sky for any sign of the parrot pirates.

Turnbuckle said, "Now that we're rid of those nasty parrot pirates, we can explore the beach on the way to pick up Keel. Hey, stop here, everyone. See that little hole in the sand, Tiller? There's a sand dollar under it."

"Wow! I bury old bones, but I didn't know that humans buried their money," said Tiller.

"He's a funny doggie," said Alee.

"It's not a real dollar. Here, let me show you," said Turnbuckle.

Turnbuckle gently scratched at the sand until a small round object appeared just below the surface. She carefully freed it from its sandy home and held it in her paw for Tiller to see.

"Gee, I've never seen one of these!" cried Tiller. "It kinda looks like a miniature frisbee. Hey, give it a toss, and I'll catch it in the air."

Turnbuckle's jaw dropped open. "What? This isn't a toy. It's a living creature."

"Oh, sorry," said Tiller with a sad face that only a wiener dog could have. "We don't have sand dollars on the Chesapeake Bay. What do you do with them?"

"Well, some people collect them, but I just like to look at them and then put them back," replied Turnbuckle.

"I like that idea," said Tiller. "Let me help you."

Tiller and Turnbuckle bent down together, placed the sand dollar back in its home, and covered it over with sand. They stood up, and Tiller scanned the beach. At the water's edge, he noticed something small and dark rolling around in an incoming wave. As the wave returned to the sea, it dropped the shapeless mass onto the sand.

Pointing in its direction, Tiller said, "Hey, Turnbuckle, something very strange looking just washed up onto the beach!"

"Let's go check it out," replied Turnbuckle. They all hurried over to the water's edge to investigate. As they bent down to get a closer look, Turnbuckle, without thinking, stretched out her paw and poked at the slimy black creature.

A black liquid squirted from the creature and covered Turnbuckle's face. She jumped up and screamed. Everyone took off running until they were a safe distance away from the scene of the attack. The five furry friends turned in time to watch the next wave roll ashore and take the creature back out to sea.

Tiller turned and looked at Turnbuckle. He held a paw up to his mouth to keep from laughing, but it didn't do any good.

"What's so funny?" she asked. Now the others were starting to giggle.

"Well," he said pointing at her, "a few minutes ago you were a calico cat. Now you are a calico cat covered with black spots!"

"Ahhh," Turnbuckle cried as she ran toward the water. She plunged into the next wave and rolled around and around until she popped back out, a calico cat once again.

"What happened?" she asked.

"It was an octopus," said Tiller, fighting back the urge to laugh. "I guess you've never been slimed by an octopus before."

"No, I haven't," she replied with a worried voice. "I've seen them, but I've never tried touching one."

"Don't worry, the octopus shoots out that black stuff when it's defending itself. It confuses its enemy and gives the octopus time to swim away," said Tiller.

"I guess I should be careful what I touch," she said sheepishly.

"Some things in the sea are okay to touch and some aren't. I learned that when I was snorkeling in the Caribbean Sea," said Tiller.

"Grandpa," said Dinghy.

"Yes, Dinghy?"

Without another word, Dinghy sprinted for the tree.

"Not again," said Rudder.

"Must be all the talk about water and snorkeling," said Anchor.

"Yeah, all you have to do is mention water and his eyes turn yellow," said Boom.

"Now Boom, don't talk about your brother that way," replied Grandpa. Dinghy raced back to the pile of puppies and jumped in, feeling much relieved.

"Ouch, that hurt," yelled Boom. "This time you landed on my tail." All the puppies laughed, especially Luff, the littlest of the litter. He loved the funny things that Dinghy did.

"Go ahead, Grandpa, I'm ready now," said Dinghy.

Grandpa just shook his head and said, "Now where was I…"

"I learned that when I was snorkeling in the Caribbean Sea," said Tiller.

"Wow, I've always wanted to explore a coral reef," said Turnbuckle. "Imagine being able to swim in crystal clear water with all those colorful fish."

"Might there be cheese on the reef?" asked Mizzen.

"I'm afraid not, Mizzen," said Tiller.

"Well then, I think I will stay here, my friend."

"We'd better get going. Keel will be getting off work soon," said Turnbuckle.

The five furry friends ran along the water's edge playing tag with the waves. Tiller turned his eyes away from the water and looked toward land. It was then that he saw a most unusual sight. It sent shivers down his long spine and made his hair stand on end. Just over a low ridge of rocks that protected the village from the sea, a whale appeared to be rising right up out of the ground.

Tiller was confused by what he saw, but he yelled out a warning anyway. "Run, everyone. There's a whale up there!"

"But, Tiller," protested Turnbuckle.

"I'll protect you. Just run away as fast as you can." With that, Tiller took off across the beach and headed for the whale. He climbed over the rocks and raced toward the creature.

"Tiller, no, it's not a real..." Turnbuckle had tried her best to warn Tiller, but it was no use. Tiller leaped at the side of the beast with teeth bared, ready to plant them in its side. When his mighty canines made contact with the flesh of the beast, the last thing Tiller expected it to be was concrete! The thunk of teeth on concrete started his body vibrating from his head all the way to his tail, which of course was a considerable distance.

Turnbuckle looked down at the poor pooch as he lay motionless on the ground.

"Oh, Tiller, are you all right?" she asked, trying to shake some life back into him. Tiller sat up dazed and looked around him with glassy eyes that had a far away look to them.

"Guess I showed him, huh!"

"You sure did, Tiller," replied Baggiewrinkle. "I don't think he will bother us any more. You scared him so much that he stopped dead in his tracks. He looks perfectly petrified."

The four of them didn't have the nerve to tell him that the whale was a concrete sculpture.

Turnbuckle helped Tiller to a wooden bench under a large tree. They sat for a few minutes until all the stars in front of Tiller's face had disappeared. "Where are we?" he asked.

"This is Neptune Park. We play here all the time," said Turnbuckle.

A look of amazement came over Tiller's face as he looked up into the tree.

"What is it, Tiller?" asked Turnbuckle.

"This tree. It looks like one of the live oaks from the tree tunnel, only this one is…gigantuous! It spreads out over the entire picnic area."

"You're right. It is a live oak," she replied, "and this is my favorite one."

Alee said, "It's a good thing that you didn't hit your head on one of these live oaks."

"I already did that, thanks to my furry friend, here," said Tiller, rubbing his head in Mizzen's direction.

"Sorry old chap. Did you know that our live oak trees were used to build the U.S.S. Constitution? The wood from the live oak is so hard that the ship was nicknamed…"

"Old Iron Sides," interrupted Tiller.

"Jolly good, old boy!"

"Mizzen, we're out of school for the summer. We don't have to learn anything," said Baggiewrinkle.

"Good grief, Baggiewrinkle," replied Mizzen, "learning does not stop just because you are out of school!"

"Mizzen is right," said Tiller. "I didn't learn about boats in school. My dad taught me, and he learned about boats when he was in the navy," replied Tiller.

"Well, that explains your propensity for the sea," said Mizzen.

Everyone stared at Mizzen.

"What?" he asked.

"There you go again with the big words," said Baggiewrinkle.

"Fine. How about talent for the sea?" asked Mizzen.

"Better," said Baggiewrinkle. "Now please stop sharing your propensity for words."

"Well done, Baggiewrinkle. As your teacher, I think you must…"

The furry group walked away and Mizzen was left talking to himself.

"Hey, wait up!" yelled Mizzen.

As they walked, Tiller heard a commotion high up in the live oaks. He looked up, and a clump of leaves landed on his face. "Ahhh!" yelled Tiller as he swatted the leaves away. "What's going on up there?"

The furry five scanned the tree tops and spotted two familiar birds flying through the thick leaves from opposite directions, unleashing a shower of green. The birds collided and fell to earth inside the shower. They lay motionless under a blanket of fallen leaves and feathers.

The furry five gathered around the pile. Tiller pushed aside the leaves and feathers and nudged both birds with his paw. "Stem, Stern. Are you alright?" Stern was lying on his back and Stem was lying on his stomach.

Stem managed to flick his wing to say yes. Baggiewrinkle noticed that Stem's beak was stuck in the ground, so he gave Stem a pull and freed it.

"Let me at em," yelled Stern. "I'll wring his skinny little neck."

"You might be too late," said Tiller, pointing to Stern.

Stem reached down and shook Stern's wings. "Stern, Stern, speak to me. Please wake up," pleaded Stem.

Stern's eyes shot open. "What happened? Where am I?"

Stem said, "Thank goodness you're alive. Now I can wring your neck!" Stem grabbed Stern around the neck and shook it.

"Wait," Stern managed to gasp. "The parrot pirates!"

Stem let go of Stern, who fell to the ground. "That's right. I forgot. We came here to warn you that two of the parrot pirates are on their way here, and they'll be here any minute."

"We have to hide," said Turnbuckle, looking around. "There," she pointed. "The library."

The furry four scurried to keep up with Turnbuckle as she darted toward a brick building a short distance from the live oak trees.

Stem and Stern staggered off toward the beach, having decided to walk, not fly. Stem thought a dip in the cool water might stop the ringing in his ears. Stern thought the cool water might stop the wringing in his neck.

The five fugitives were nearly at the steps of the library when Tiller looked over his shoulder and saw brightly colored feathers fly past the lighthouse. "Quickly! They're almost here," he shouted.

The furry five burst through the library door to a warning of "Shhhhh!" from the librarian at the desk. They scattered and disappeared into the stacks of books.

Tiller and Turnbuckle just happened to turn down the mystery aisle. "This looks like a great place to hide. Those nasty parrot pirates will never find us in here. They couldn't solve a mystery if their lives depended on it," said Turnbuckle.

The large window next to the mystery aisle would be the perfect place for the parrot pirates to spot Tiller and Turnbuckle, so they ducked under it and flattened themselves against the wall. Seconds later, they heard the flapping of wings and a plunk, plunk outside on the window sill. "The parrot pirates are right over top of us," whispered Tiller.

"Are you sure they didn't see us?" Turnbuckle whispered back.

"Not really," said Tiller, focusing on two long bird shadows dancing like ghosts across the mystery books a few feet away.

Tiller and Turnbuckle could hear the buccaneer birds' muffled conversation through the window. The birds were pacing back and forth on the window sill, scanning the inside of the library. "Why did we land here?"

"Because, I thought I saw something white and furry run into the library."

"How can you see anything with that patch over your eye? I told you not to fly with that thing. You almost ran into the lighthouse. I don't see anyone inside the library. Let's get out of here. They wouldn't be here, anyway. Cats and dogs wouldn't know how to read a book if their lives depended on it. Let's go ask those two goofy seagulls if they saw anything."

Tiller and Turnbuckle heard the flapping of wings and relaxed. "Boy, that was close," said Turnbuckle.

Tiller looked around and was pleasantly surprised at how cozy the small library felt. It was so unlike the large ones that he was used to in the big city. It had an old book smell that he really liked. "I could spend all day in here," whispered Tiller.

"So could I," replied Turnbuckle, "if we didn't have a boat to find."

"Maybe after we find Dogspeed, we could read a book together," said Tiller.

"Sounds perfect," said Turnbuckle. "Or should I say 'purrfect'?"

"This is not going to be a perfect day, my friends, until we find Dogspeed," said Mizzen who had caught up with them by hopping across several shelves of books.

"He's right, Tiller," agreed Turnbuckle. "We'd better get going."

On the way out of the library, Turnbuckle asked Tiller, "What kind of stories do you like to read?"

"I love a good mystery. My favorite is *The Hardy Boys*."

"What a small world, my furry friend. My favorite is *The Nancy Drew Mysteries*," said Turnbuckle.

The other furry friends had already gathered at the door. Mizzen said, "I made a complete search of the park and the parrot pirates are nowhere in sight."

"You didn't happen to see Nancy Drew out there, did you?" asked Turnbuckle.

"Excuse me?" replied Mizzen.

"Never mind."

Once outside the library, Turnbuckle announced, "Keep a sharp eye out for any feathered buccaneers on our way to the 4th of May."

"Wow! You're able to time travel here in Georgia?" asked Tiller.

"Of course not, funny doggie," replied Turnbuckle. "The 4th of May is a café on Mallery Street in the village. That's where we're going to pick up Keel. She works there. Keel is a tiny white Pomeranian ball of energy that runs like the wind and can bark with the best of them."

"You know, my little stomach isn't feeling so perfect," said Mizzen. "It is telling me that some food would enable it to achieve perfection."

"Can't you just say you're hungry," replied Baggiewrinkle.

"That works, too."

"Come on," said Turnbuckle. "Maybe Keel will fix us a treat."

That's all Mizzen had to hear. He took off down Mallery Street and Baggiewrinkle and Alee followed him.

"Hey, Tiller, before we go to the 4th of May, I want to introduce you to a tree."

"That's okay," said Tiller. "I don't have to go to the bathroom right now."

"That's not why I want to introduce you to this tree, silly. I want to introduce you because this is no ordinary tree."

"You know, I'm getting the feeling that nothing on this island is ordinary," said Tiller.

Turnbuckle just smiled and continued walking until they stood at the base of another large, live oak tree. In a flash, Turnbuckle leaped six feet up into the tree and sat comfortably between two large branches. "Notice anything unusual about this tree?" asked Turnbuckle.

It was then that Tiller noticed a human face carved in the tree just below where Turnbuckle was sitting. Remembering his earlier experience with the whale, he made a quick decision not to attack the tree. "Don't move, Turnbuckle," said Tiller nervously. "I'll get help."

"Hold on there, hairy knight in shining armor. This is Tom, the tree spirit," said Turnbuckle.

"Oh, great," said Tiller, looking around, "a tree spirit. What could be scary about this island?"

Using her sharp claws, Turnbuckle nimbly walked down the bark of the tree. "Don't worry, my stretched-out friend. The tree spirits are harmless."

"Spirits? You mean there are more of them?"

"Oh, yes. A human carved several of these faces on oak trees around the island."

"Why did he do that?"

"My mom told me it was because he just wanted to say thank you to all the sailors who had lost their lives at sea aboard the sailing ships made from St. Simons oak."

"That's a great way to say thank you. I think I'm going to like these tree spirits," said Tiller.

"I thought you would, since you are a sailor. I love the tree spirits. They make me feel safe. I named this one Tom; he's my favorite. When I was little, I spent hours in this tree hiding from humans and talking to Tom. He has always been like a friend."

"I always talk to the birds, and the sky, and the fish, and the water," said Tiller. "They're my friends."

"It's nice to have friends to talk to," replied Turnbuckle.

"Yeah, and with a friend you can always have adventures together."

"Like we're having now," exclaimed Turnbuckle.

"Hey, how would you like to go on some sailing adventures with me?" asked Tiller. "I sure could use a first mate to help me sail Dogspeed."

"For real?"

"You betcha."

"But I don't know too much about sailing," said Turnbuckle.

"I'll teach you," said Tiller.

"Wow, I've always dreamed of having adventures out in the world. Imagine me sailing the ocean blue," said Turnbuckle with a far away look in her eye.

"Now all we have to do is find Dogspeed," said Tiller.

"That's where our friends come in. Last one to the 4th of May is a rotten egg."

Turnbuckle took off down Mallery Street.

"I'm getting way too much exercise," Tiller said to Tom.

Chapter Nine

The Pier and the Pelican

The 4th of May sat on the corner of Ocean Boulevard and Mallery Street. The first thing Tiller saw when he and Turnbuckle arrived at the café was the crowd of humans dining under the shade of a bright green and white awning that wrapped around the outside of the building. Tiller and Turnbuckle weaved past the line of humans in the doorway. Once inside the 4th of May, Turnbuckle spotted Baggiewrinkle, Alee, and Mizzen admiring the assorted sweets in the dessert case. Keel was cleaning the floor with her bushy white tail. The five furry friends walked over to Keel and stood watching her go around and around in circles.

"Someone should stop her before she cleans a hole all the way to China," said Alee.

"Hi, Keel," said Turnbuckle.

This startled Keel, and she started barking so loudly that everyone in the café stared at her.

"Oh my, you just scared the biscuits out of me. What in the ham sandwich are you all doing here?"

"Keel, I'd like you to meet my new friend, Tiller. I'm giving him a tour of the island," said Turnbuckle. "He just sailed here from the Chesa...the Chesa..."

"The Chesapeake!" said Keel.

"Say, how come everyone else knows that word?" questioned Turnbuckle.

"That's okay, Turnbuckle," said Tiller. "It's a tricky word. You'll get it soon."

Tiller shook paws with Keel. "Nice to meet you, Keel," said Tiller.

"Likewise," replied Keel. "Say, that was a long way to sail. You must be starving."

"Yes, he is," said Mizzen. "And he loves cheese, any kind of cheese."

"Well, I'll fix you all a little surprise," said Keel, "and we'll go to the pier to eat."

"Yes!" Mizzen cried out.

With treats in hand, Keel led the way past the many shops and restaurants that lined Mallery Street in the village. The aroma of homemade biscuits filled the air. At the end of the street was the long concrete fishing pier that stood high over the water. Humans crowded each side of the pier, holding onto fishing poles, hoping to catch dinner. The smell in the air quickly turned fishy. The six furry friends threaded their way through the mass of tackle boxes and buckets of bait. Seagulls squawked overhead, hoping for a handout. Two of the gulls seemed to take particular interest in the six and followed them down the pier. Tiller noticed that one of them kept looking backward, causing him to fly into the other gull. He smiled as his two friends, Stem and Stern, landed on the railing just ahead of the six. Stem faced the pier and Stern faced the water.

Tiller let out a little bark and twirled around. "Stem, Stern! It's so good to see you again, my friends. I hope you are feeling better after your crash."

"Much better, thank you," said Stern, rubbing his neck. "It's good to see…"

"Stern! You can't see him if you're facing the water. Turn around," said Stem.

"Oh, sorry. Ah, there you are," Stern said. "It's good to see you again, my wiener friend."

Stern started laughing.

"Why are you laughing?" asked Tiller.

"Because you're in for a big surprise," said Stern.

Stem hit Stern with his wing and said, "He means... ah... that we're surprised to see our long dog friend here on our pier."

Stern started again. "Say, did I mention that..."

Before Stern could finish, Stem swatted Stern, knocking him off the railing. They both flew off in opposite directions.

Tiller turned to Turnbuckle and asked, "What was that all about?"

"Oh. Don't pay attention to those two; they've been flying in circles too long."

As they continued down the pier, Tiller sensed a shift in the wind. He looked to the sky as gray clouds over the ocean thickened and raced their way. The wind suddenly grew stronger and the air got noticeably cooler. "Here we go again," thought Tiller.

When the six shivering friends arrived at the very end of the pier, they all sat, eyes wide open, waiting for the treat to be opened. Keel lifted the lid to reveal a plate of steamed vegetables. Tiller's jaw dropped in disappointment, Baggiewrinkle covered his head with his paws, and Mizzen fell backward off the pier, disappearing into the churning water below.

"There he is," said Turnbuckle, pointing to a small, furry white spot that had bobbed to the surface.

"Mizzen, are you okay?" yelled Tiller.

Mizzen tried to speak, but the strong currents kept pulling him under.

Tiller heard a whooshing sound and looked up into the dark clouds just in time to see a large, gray pelican circling overhead.

"Mizzen!" shouted Tiller, pointing to the sky. "Look out!"

Mizzen looked up. The pelican folded back his enormous wings and went into a dive, straight toward Mizzen. With only a split second to react, Mizzen dove underwater. The others watched in horror as Mizzen disappeared below the surface with the pelican crashing through the water only seconds later. The huge bird resurfaced, put his mighty wings to work, and lifted off into the sky. Five furry faces looked on, helplessly, as the great bird flew out to sea with their friend.

"Oh no, poor Mizzen," sighed Turnbuckle.

"Grandpa," said Dinghy.
"Not again, Dinghy," replied Grandpa.

"No Grandpa. Luff is crying."

"Now, Luff, don't cry," said Grandpa.

"But Mizzen was my favorite. I don't want him to die."

"I know you don't, Luff, but I have to tell the story the way it happened," said Grandpa. "Be a big boy so I can finish the story."

"Okay, Grandpa. I'll be a big boy."

"That's my big Luff," Grandpa said, patting Luff on the head. "Now, where was I...?"

"Oh no, poor Mizzen," sighed Turnbuckle.

"I'm going to miss the little guy," said Alee, frowning.

"I'm even going to miss his big words," said Baggiewrinkle. "Too bad pelicans like to eat mice instead of vegetables."

The furry five sat silently, looking out over the water.

A hungry grackle bird looking for leftovers landed on the railing and said, "Sorry about your friend. I saw the whole thing from the air. Wow! Not a pretty sight." After a few moments of silence, the grackle bird asked, "Is anybody going to eat those veggies?" Tiller and Baggiewinkle made a grab for the bird, but he was able to escape their grasp.

"Scavenger!" they yelled as he flew off.

Tiller was still looking skyward when he spotted a large familiar bird flying toward them.

"Tell me that isn't what I think it is," said Tiller, squinting.

"I think it is," said Turnbuckle.

As the large familiar bird flew closer, they noticed a small white spot on its back. The bird circled over the pier, and the furry five could see the small white spot more clearly. It wasn't a small white spot at all; it was a small white creature holding onto the bird's back with one paw, the other raised in the air, yelling, "Yahoo!"

The flying duo landed on the wooden railing. The creature jumped off the pelican's back and yelled, "Now that was an awesome ride, dude!"

"Mizzen!" the five yelled. "You're alive!" They grabbed Mizzen and hugged him until his eyes bulged.

"We thought you were a goner. What happened?" asked Tiller.

"Well, let me start by introducing my friend. Everyone, this is Poopdeck the Pelican."

"Nice to meet you, Poopdeck," said the five. They all shook Poopdeck's wing.

"It's nice to meet all of you. Mizzen told me about you while we were flying," said Poopdeck.

"It was thrilling," said Mizzen. "I had never been flying before. The view of St. Simons Island was most spectacular."

"But, Mizzen, how did you survive… you know, being eaten by Poopdeck?" asked Keel.

"Oh, that was easy. Tell them Poopdeck."

"Well, I happened to be flying by when I saw this furry white creature fall into the water. That's when I decided to put my diving skills to use, for diving is what we pelicans do."

"Correct!" added Mizzen excitedly. "So, he scooped me up and flew to a big green buoy with a loud bell on it where I could rest. He told me that he only meant to rescue me, not eat me. Tell them why you did not eat me."

"Because, well, unlike most pelicans, I'm a...a vegetarian."

"Jolly lucky for me," said Mizzen. "After all, my goal in life is to eat snacks, not become a snack."

"Speaking of snacks, what are we going to do with all these vegetables?" asked Keel.

Poopdeck interrupted, "I think I can help." The six looked on as Poopdeck picked up the tray of veggies and tilted it toward his large gullet. The veggies slid down his long neck. "All gone," he said.

Feeling relieved that he didn't have to eat the vegetables, Tiller said, "Poopdeck, I don't know how to thank you."

Poopdeck smiled and said, "Anytime, my canine friend. Well, I think my work here is done." The great bird spread his wings, lifted off the pier, and flew out to sea.

The six furry friends waved goodbye. "I hope we'll get to see Poopdeck again one day," said Tiller.

"We will," said Mizzen, "as long as Keel is fixing the treats."

"Now that we are all together, are we ready to continue our quest to find the parrot pirates?" asked Turnbuckle.

"You bet," replied Tiller.

"I shall lead the way to the scallywags," said a determined Mizzen.

"He does have a way with words," said Keel.

The six furry friends made their way back across the park, past the library, past the whale, and past Turnbuckle's favorite live oak tree. Tiller stopped and turned around, looking back on the park. "Hey, Turnbuckle, why is this called Neptune Park?"

"Do you like history, Tiller?"

"You bet I do!"

"Well, you've come to the right island," she said. "St. Simons is full of history."

"Yeah, and full of pirates, too," said Keel.

"Keel, the pirates can wait one more minute," said Mizzen. "Continue, Turnbuckle."

"Tiller, imagine that it's the 1860s. The Civil War is raging and many slaves live and work here on the island's plantations. One of those slaves is named Neptune Small. He grew up with Henry Lord Page King, the son of the plantation owner. But you can call him Lordy. That's what Neptune called him. Neptune and Lordy were like brothers. They played together all the time, and they always looked out for each other. Even when they grew up and Lordy left the plantation to serve in the Confederate Army, Neptune went with him.

"One day, after a terrible battle in Fredericksburg, Lordy didn't return to camp. So, Neptune went to search for him. He wandered the battlefield looking for his beloved friend, and when he found him, Captain Henry Lord Page King lay dead. Neptune carried Lordy off the battlefield in his arms and placed him in a wagon.

"Then Neptune did an amazing thing. He walked beside that wagon, beside his friend, for five hundred miles until he had returned Lordy to the King family for burial.

"After the war, the slaves were freed, and the King family was so grateful to Neptune that they gave him a plot of land where he and his family spent the rest of their lives. We're standing on that plot of land." Turnbuckle noticed that Tiller's eyes looked a bit misty.

"Wow, that's a wonderful story of friendship," said Tiller. "I'm glad that they named this park after Neptune. It makes this place very special."

"I agree, my sensitive friend," replied Turnbuckle.

Chapter Ten

On to the Hangout

"So, Turnbuckle, where are we headed?" asked Tiller as the furry friends continued along Ocean Boulevard.

"To the hangout of the Parrot Pirate Gang. It's called Bloody Marsh," she replied.

Tiller stopped in his tracks and looked at Turnbuckle. "Not another marsh," he said nervously. "My first trip to a marsh almost turned out to be bloody."

"It's okay," said Keel. "This marsh hasn't been that bloody, lately."

"That bloody, lately!" roared Tiller.

"Well, once in a while the parrot pirates get a little carried away with the tourists, but they don't usually bother the locals too much," said Mizzen.

"Why is it called Bloody Marsh?" asked Tiller.

Turnbuckle explained, "A long time ago, humans from England built a fort on the banks of the Frederica River."

"Naturally," said Mizzen, "they called it Fort Frederica, seeing how the English are so clever. A few years later Spanish humans sneaked up here from Florida and got into a fight with the English...put 'em up, come on put 'em up!" cried Mizzen out of the blue.

"Mizzen!" yelled Keel. This seemed to bring Mizzen back to reality.

"Oh, sorry. For a moment I thought I was an English soldier," said Mizzen proudly.

"Anyway, as I was saying, the Spanish humans had gotten into a fight with the English humans, and they attacked the fort."

"That's right, but some of the Spanish soldiers decided to rest in a marsh," added Baggiewrinkle. "While they were resting, the English soldiers attacked them, and lots of Spanish soldiers were killed or wounded."

Mizzen abruptly fell on the ground and played dead.

Turnbuckle shook her head and continued, "Anyway, this became known as the Battle of Bloody Marsh because the marsh ran red with the blood of the dead and wounded."

Mizzen popped back up, shook his body, and cried, "Yuck, blood, eeuw, aah!"

They stared at Mizzen until he stopped.

Tiller said, "Mizzen, this is a serious matter. This marsh sounds like a perfect hideout for a gang of blood-thirsty pirates."

The six furry friends continued on, gathering courage with each step. By the time they reached the marsh they had transformed into the six fearsome furry friends.

They turned off the road onto a narrow path that led into the marsh. Turnbuckle raised a paw into the air for quiet. With his nose to the ground, Tiller sharpened his senses. The six began to slink along in silence for what seemed like an eternity, until only moments later, they found themselves standing at the edge of a clearing.

"This is Bloody Marsh," whispered Turnbuckle.

"Looks deserted to me," Tiller whispered back.

"Let's check out the place," suggested Keel.

"That is a good idea because something doesn't seem right. I smell a rat," said Mizzen.

"Too bad," replied Tiller, "I was hoping for a parrot."

The six fearsome furry friends stepped cautiously into the clearing looking for any sign of the dreaded Parrot Pirate Gang. Tiller said, "I don't think anyone is..."

Tiller froze as a hood was thrust over his head. He finished his sentence with a muffled..."here!"

"Oh, we are here all right," said a voice that sounded like a pirate from the Caribbean. "Welcome to Bloody Marsh, matey!"

"Is this Skipper the Sparrow?" asked Tiller through the hood.

"No. D'name is Pearl."

"Pearl?"

"Dat is right. Pearl the Parrot Pirate."

"That has a nice ring to it," said Tiller.

"Tank you," said Pearl. "I got dat name from d'pearl ring I took off the last landlubber who tried to find our hideout."

"Oh!" said Tiller nervously.

"And soon my friend, Black Beak d' Parrot Pirate, will join us," said Pearl.

"Black Beak and Pearl?" Tiller questioned. "Those names sound familiar. Did you ever hang out with a bunch of pirates in the Caribbean?"

"I tink you 'ave been watchin' too many movies, matey. Now enough wid d'introductions, we mus' get movin'."

"But what about Turnbuckle and the rest of my friends?" asked Tiller.

"Never mind 'bout them. Just keep walkin', and nobody gets hurt," replied Pearl.

"Mr. Pearl, am I being... shanghaied?"

"Yes. You are being taken for crew by unscrupulous means."

"Say, that sounds familiar. Do you know a mouse named Mizzen?" asked Tiller.

"Ah, well, no. I, ah, don't know who you are talkin' 'bout. No more talkin' now, jus' walk."

"But, Mr. Pearl, if Bloody Marsh is your hangout, where are we headed?"

"Dat would be to d'odder hangout, Fort Frederica."

"Did you say Fort Featherica?"

"No. It's Frederica. Although I like d' sound of Featherica for a gang of parrot pirates," replied Pearl.

"Is that where you've taken my boat?"

"If you are a good doggie an' do what I say, you might jus' find your boat and your friends at Fort Frederica. Dat is where we will meet up wid Skipper the Sparrow an' d'res' o' d'gang," Pearl replied.

The two trudged silently from the marsh. Tiller stumbled and tripped several times and even smacked his head on a live oak. He noticed, through the hood, that it was getting dark. Suddenly, Tiller felt a cold sharp talon on his shoulder. "Stop," demanded Pearl. "We are meeting Black Beak here at Christ Church. He is in d'cemetery placing a potted plant at a pirate's plot."

"Wait a minute. Do you mean Black Beak the Parrot Pirate is putting flowers on the grave of a pirate?" asked Tiller.

"Well, you could put it dat way, but it does not sound as poetic," replied Pearl.

"True. It doesn't have the same ring to it, especially coming from a poetic parrot pirate," said Tiller.

"Are you trying to get on my good side, wise weiner?"

"Can't hurt. I thought it might help get this hood off my head?"

"Well," said Pearl, "since we are at d'cemetery, I tink 'tis safe to take it off now." After Pearl removed the hood, Tiller took a big breath of fresh air and shook his head back and forth the way dogs do. Seeing Pearl for the first time, Tiller couldn't help noticing the red feathers sticking out the top of his head.

"What are you looking at?" bellowed Pearl.

"Oh… ah… I was just looking at the church behind you," replied Tiller, pointing over Pearl's shoulder to the church silhouetted in the moonlight. "Wow, Christ Church is beautiful."

Tiller's quick thinking seemed to distract Pearl. "'Tis beautiful in the moonlight, but d'graveyard is scary in d'moonlight," he said. Tiller thought he detected a slight bit of nervousness in Pearl's voice.

"Come on now, Mr. Pearl. What could be scary about this island?" asked Tiller. "So, are there any famous people buried here?"

"Of course. Right down dere is d'King family."

"You mean the King family from the time of the Civil War?"

"Say, you know your history. Not bad for a wayward wiener."

"Thank you very much," replied Tiller.

"An' jus' a few steps over dere is the famous writer, Eugenia Price. She wrote many works o' fiction 'bout life here on St. Simon's Islan'."

"Well, you're quite the literary scholar. Not bad for a parrot pirate," said Tiller.

"Tank you very much."

"I suppose this place is full of ghosts," said Tiller.

"Yes, an' dat is exactly why we are gettin' out o' here as soon as we find Black Beak," replied Pearl. "Dat parrot mus' be around here somewhere."

Suddenly, there came a rustling, a thump, and a voice screeching something from the bushes near them.

Tiller's four paws left the ground at the same time. His little legs began to spin before he even hit the ground. Once he made contact, he was off and running.

"Where do you tink you are goin' my weirded out wiener friend?"

"How about another island with no ghosts!" said Tiller.

"Keep your fur on, pooch. Dat was no ghost. Dat was jus' Black Beak. He does not fly too well in d'dark wid d'patch ovah his eye."

Black Beak stood up and shook himself off the way birds do. A few feathers were out of place, but only his pride was hurt.

"Nice of you to drop in, Black Beak," said Pearl. "How did it go wid d' potted plant?"

"Awk!" screeched Black Beak. "Positively peachy."

"Peachy?" questioned Tiller. "You don't sound much like a pirate to me."

"Awk! Excuse me. Argh, positively peachy, matey! Is that better?"

"Alright, we don' have time for dis," said Pearl.

"Awk! Sorry," said Black Beak. "But your canine companion has been watching too many movies."

"I know. I told 'em d'same ting," replied Pearl.

"Hey, I can't help it if your feathered friend sounds more like a Caribbean canary than a parrot pirate!" said Tiller.

"Awk! Watch it, will ya? Pirates have feelings too, you know."

"You're right, Black Beak," replied Tiller. "I'm sorry, it's just that I'm not used to being around pirates. I didn't know they could be so sensitive."

"I tink you will find dat we are no ordinary pirates," said Pearl.

"I should have known," said Tiller. "By the way, Black Beak, isn't your patch supposed to be over your left eye?"

"Oh...ah...yes...must a shifted in the crash." Black Beak moved the patch from his right eye to his left eye.

Pearl said, "Now, we will need to be movin'. Skipper the Sparrow is waitin' for you. He is looking forward to making you a crewmember on the newest boat in his fleet."

Black Beak flew on ahead to announce their arrival to Skipper. As he weaved his way through the thick stands of live oaks, Pearl and Tiller could hear rustling, thumping, and a voice screeching something.

Pearl just shook his head and said, "Dat boy is going to break his beak one day."

Looking for a way out of the graveyard, Pearl and Tiller both realized that they would need to walk past dozens of headstones. As they tiptoed past several graves, a sudden rush of warm air overtook them.

"Did you feel that?" asked Tiller.

Pearl didn't answer. He stood, still as stone, staring a few feet ahead. A flame had suddenly begun to flicker in front of a headstone, casting an eerie glow.

Pearl's eyes doubled in size and his tail feathers began to shake uncontrollably. He tried to scream, but his opened beak remained silent. He flapped his parrot wings as fast as he could and flew high into the night sky, never looking back at that cemetery.

Oddly, Tiller was not scared by the presence of the flame. He found himself drawn to it. The closer he got, the calmer he felt. Tiller sat and stared past the flame into the headstone. "Rachel Lanier," read Tiller. "I wonder who she was." As he sat, deep in thought, he found comfort in the flame's glow and hoped that Rachel did, too.

Tiller stood and, stepping around the headstone, gazed into the darkness. He let out a little bark and said, "I'm no longer afraid of the darkness, or of the parrot pirates, or of anything."

Earlier, Tiller had thought about escaping, but it seemed hopeless because Pearl was guarding him so closely. Now, Tiller's escape would be easy. He simply walked off into the woods in search of Dogspeed.

Chapter Eleven

The Search

"I hope I have better luck this time, with my excellent sense of direction," said Tiller to the live oaks. "That fort can't be too far from here."

He looked around for something that might point him in the right direction. The woods ahead grew more and more dense, blocking his way, so he turned slightly to the right and walked for several minutes. That's when Tiller saw the woods coming to an end. He quickened his pace. In his excitement, however, he did not notice a large clump of Spanish moss hanging from the low branch of a live oak and became hopelessly tangled in it. "Yuck!" he said, spitting moss everywhere. "It's pretty to look at, but it sure doesn't taste good," he bellowed, still struggling. "And it doesn't feel so good in my ears."

Tiller let out a huge sneeze. "Or up my nose!"

Picking the last bit of moss from his nose, Tiller continued on his way, happy to leave the moss and the live oaks behind. A few minutes later, he stood at the edge of the woods looking at a familiar sight. "Not another forest of ferns. No offense, ferns, but the last time I walked through you, I almost became a snack."

Tiller turned to walk the other way, but something made him stop. "These ferns may lead to a marsh, like last time, and the marsh will lead to the river, which is where I will find Dogspeed. So, it makes sense to follow the ferns. Besides, what are the odds that I will run into Gunwale the Gator, again. Even if I do, I'm not afraid of him anymore. Okay ferns, ready or not, here I come."

Tiller plowed through the dense forest of ferns, in the dark, unafraid. The deeper into the forest he walked, the cooler it became and a light mist covered the ground. Tiller felt his paws sinking, only slightly at first, as the ground became softer and softer. The air grew even cooler, and the mist rose from the ground, making it hard to see. Tiller considered stopping; instead, he took one step too many. All four of his paws sank deep into thick gooey mud. No matter how much he wiggled and pulled, the swamp's mucky anchor would not let him go. He shivered in the cool air as the mist swirled around him, imprisoning him in a thick fog. Tiller was all alone. At least that's what he thought.

"Well, well. What do we have here?" called a voice from the fog.

Tiller couldn't see who it was, but he recognized the menacing voice. There was a moment of silence and the voice came again, closer this time. "It's my favorite long dog back for another adventure in the marsh."

"I'm not afraid of you, Gunwale," said Tiller.

"Oh, well that's good. I find that the more relaxed dinner is the more tender it is."

Gunwale was now close enough for Tiller to smell his bad breath. The familiar odor of stale swamp water filled Tiller's nostrils and made his eyes water. "I wouldn't come any closer if I were you," said Tiller.

"Hssssssssssss," Gunwale hissed in reply.

Tiller knew he was about to strike. "Errrrrrrrrrrr," growled Tiller with his jaws open and ready.

Gunwale's long green jaws materialized out of the fog, but just as they began to open, they suddenly snapped shut. Gunwale's eyes opened wide as he caught sight of something over Tiller's shoulder. "Ahhhhhhh," screamed Gunwale. He turned and thrashed his way back into the fog.

"Hah! I showed him. I bet that's the last anyone will ever see…" Tiller stopped when he realized that the fog had become much brighter, as though a light were shining into it from over his shoulder. With all four paws still stuck in the mud, Tiller managed to turn his head enough to see a most unusual sight behind him. A few feet away sat a beautiful human lady on a large white horse. The long white gown she was wearing draped onto the horse, and light from the lantern she was holding pierced the fog. Tiller couldn't decide which was making the fog brighter, the light from the lantern or the kindness radiating from her face. All he could do was stare at the amazing sight.

In silence, the lady, who seemed to glow, reached down from her horse, placed her hand under Tiller's belly, and carefully scooped him out of the mud. It was almost as if he were being lifted by a gentle force rather than a hand. The lady motioned with her head, as if imploring him to follow; she turned the horse and rode slowly into the fog.

With the lantern's light to guide him, Tiller followed the lady for several minutes. He felt the same sense of comfort that he had felt from the flame, earlier.

Then, as suddenly as it had come, the fog lifted. The lady raised her lantern and pointed with it. Before Tiller could thank her for releasing him from his swampy prison, she vanished with the last wisps of fog.

Unable to believe his eyes, Tiller said, simply, "Thank you, lady."

He walked, confidently, in the direction she had pointed with the lantern. Tiller jumped and gave a little bark, for the moon had suddenly danced out from behind the clouds, and its light revealed a grassy meadow ahead. "Now this is more like it," said Tiller to the moon.

Tiller rolled over in the cool grass. He wiggled his long body back and forth, and, after a good scratch, just lay there, gazing at the stars. He loved to look for his favorite constellations. Tiller could spend hours lying on the deck of Dogspeed imagining himself up there playing among the stars. "Hello my friend, Draco. Hello my friend, Hercules. And how are you tonight, Mr. Dipper?"

Tiller noticed the North Star and jumped up. "Goodness, Mr. Dipper, you've just pointed me to the North Star. I was so happy being with you, I almost forgot about Dogspeed. I have to keep heading north to find her."

Tiller pranced across the meadow until his long snout trapped a familiar smell. He stopped, lifted his head, and took another long sniff. "Salt air. I smell a salty river, Mr. Moon. I'll bet it's the Frederica River."

With his sniffer leading the way, Tiller ran as fast as he could. Soon the meadow gave way to live oaks with Spanish moss, palm trees, magnolia trees, and crepe myrtle trees, each with a bed of ferns at its feet. Tiller excitedly dodged the trees and scooted under the ferns.

Standing on his hind paws, Tiller peeked over the ferns for yet another long sniff. "I'm very close," he said to the ferns.

That's when he saw the glow. A few hundred yards ahead, the night sky was lit up just enough for him to see the outline of a sailboat's mast. "Yes! I have found the parrot pirate hideout. Hang in there, Dogspeed, I'm coming," he whispered. Tiller imagined Skipper the Sparrow and the parrots sitting on Dogspeed, lanterns flickering, plotting his recapture.

"I must have a plan," he thought. Just then, he heard a rustling, a thump, and a voice screeching something.

"Not again," Tiller whispered to the ferns. "Black Beak has returned, but this time, my feathered friend, I won't be so easy to capture."

Tiller tiptoed off, under cover of the ferns.

Rustle, thump, screech!

Tiller changed direction.

Rustle, thump, screech!

Tiller changed direction.

With each rustle, thump, and screech, Black Beak got closer. "Come on, Tiller. I know you're out there," echoed Black Beak's voice in the night air. "Please make this easy on me so I don't break my beak."

Tiller changed direction one more time, slinking away under the ferns. A few moments later, he stopped, raised his head, and listened–nothing. "See ya, Black Beak," he muttered.

Lowering his head, Tiller took one more step. That's when he nearly bumped into the wall. He managed to stop one nose length away, which, of course was still a safe distance. Tiller took a step back. Scanning the eight foot long, two foot high barrier, he discovered that it was part of a larger structure. He could now see a curved roof reaching a height of about four feet in the middle. "Looks like it's made of brick," Tiller thought.

He reached out his paw and touched the cold hard obstruction. "Yep. It's brick alright," he whispered to himself. "Moss-covered brick. Very old moss-covered brick. Even the roof is brick." Walking along the length of it, Tiller wondered what it had been used for. "Looks like it was a small shelter," he thought. Reaching the end of it, Tiller stopped and peeked around the corner to discover an opening in the front. It was dark inside. "A perfect hiding spot," he thought.

He listened for a few seconds–no sound from inside. Tiller…slowly…tip…toed…in. After brushing the spider webs from his face, he turned around to face the opening and lay on the cold dirt floor, waiting to pounce on Black Beak should he appear. Suddenly, his nose filled with mildew hanging in the dank air; he covered his face with his paws, just in time, to prevent a huge sneeze. "That was a close one," he thought. "If I can just stay quiet, no one will ever find me in here."

"Do you visit this tomb very often?" came a gruff voice behind Tiller.

"Yeeeeoooooooowwww!" yelled Tiller, jumping up and smacking his head into the brick ceiling.

The crack on the head stunned Tiller just long enough for a blindfold to be placed over his eyes. He stood and shook off the cobwebs.

Tiller heard a rustle, a thump, and a screech just outside the opening. "Nice work directing Tiller to the tomb, Black Beak."

"Thank you, oh great Sparrow."

Tiller felt Skipper's warm breath on his neck. "Welcome to the Old Burial Grounds, Tiller. Now, the way I see it, you can stay here in this old tomb, which I don't think you want to do. Or, you can come with us to the hideout, peaceful like. It's just a short walk through the fort; if you're a good doggie, and don't try any tricks, I won't have to use my silver dagger."

With a few cobwebs still lingering in his head, Tiller toddled out of the tomb, and the three marched to the fort in silence.

Chapter Twelve

The Surprise

Skipper stopped at the entrance to the fort. "Watch your step, doggie," he said. "We're about to walk over a mound of earth. It's all that's left of the fort's walls."

Once over the mound, they walked in silence for a few minutes. Suddenly, Tiller tripped and fell over something hard sticking out of the ground. He rolled over in the grass a few times and fell off what felt like a wall onto a dirt floor a few feet below.

"Sorry doggie, I should have warned you about that brick foundation you tripped over, but if you had to trip and fall, landing in Doctor Hawkins' basement is as good a place as any," said Skipper.

Black Beak laughed and said, "What's left of the doctor's basement, that is. Doctor Hawkins and his house have been gone for over two hundred years."

Skipper stretched out a wing and Tiller grabbed on, pulling himself out of the basement; a few minutes later, they arrived at the remains of a small stone building by the river where ammunition had once been stored. Skipper put a wing on Tiller's shoulder, stopping him. "Here we are," said Skipper. "This is the hideout of the Parrot Pirate Gang."

Tiller stood still and listened and sniffed. He could hear water gently lapping on the shore, so he knew he was standing next to the Frederica River. He recognized the sound of Dogspeed's halyard clanging softly in the gentle breeze. The place had a soggy smell after a century of moss and decay.

"Black Beak, would you be kind enough to escort Mr. Tiller below deck on Dogspeed?" Skipper ordered.

"Aye, Aye, your Skipperness."

"Make sure his blindfold stays nice and tight and that he doesn't have a mind to escape."

"Awk! There will be no escaping tonight," said Black Beak as he guided Tiller onto the deck of Dogspeed and directed him down the hatch.

It felt good to be back on Dogspeed, even if Tiller couldn't see her. He sat in silence with Black Beak.

A conversation, on deck, between Skipper and Pearl was making him very nervous.

"What shall we do wid Tiller?" asked Pearl.

"Before we have him do back-breaking work on Dogspeed, we'd better make him walk the plank to teach him a lesson," replied Skipper.

"An excellent idea, your Seaworthiness."

"Black Beak," yelled Skipper. "Bring Tiller on deck and stand him by the railing."

"Coming, your Skipperhood." Black Beak prodded Tiller up on deck and stood him by the railing.

Skipper the Sparrow spoke. "Now walk."

Tiller took one small step out on the wobbly plank and stopped. "Any chance I can get one last dog biscuit?"

"No talking," commanded Skipper. "My silver dagger is close to your back. Now, take one more step."

Tiller obeyed, slowly slipping one paw forward until he felt the end of the plank.

"Well done, doggie," said Skipper. "Now there's only one thing left to do."

"Is this where I get to make my phone call?"

"No phone call. Just take off your blindfold. There is something you need to see before you jump."

Tiller nervously reached up for the blindfold and slowly pulled it off his head. In the moment that it took his eyes to adjust to the dim light of lanterns hanging on shore, he heard a loud, "SURPRISE!"

Tiller rubbed his eyes and then dropped his jaw in amazement to see Turnbuckle, Baggiewrinkle, Alee, Mizzen, and Keel, standing together on shore, smiling. Two familiar looking seagulls were sitting on Dogspeed. Stem was on the front and Stern was on the back. "Say, what's going on?" asked Tiller.

Skipper the Sparrow put away his dagger and spoke. "Well, matey, now that you can see, let me introduce myself. I am Skipper the Sparrow, and we are the Parrot Pirate Gang. We are harmless parrots just pretending to be pirates. It's more of a... club. We travel around the island together having fun and playing jokes."

Tiller felt so relieved that they were not real pirates, his tail came out from between his legs. He said to Turnbuckle, "So I suppose you were in on this little joke."

"I sure was. Remember when I had that talk with Mizzen behind St. Simons Elementary School? That's when we hatched this whole plan. You see, Skipper the Sparrow left out one important thing. The parrot pirates not only have fun and play jokes, they also help people. When Mizzen told Skipper the Sparrow about the rip in your sail, the Skipper wanted to fix it for you. Of course, he wanted to have a little fun, too."

"Boy, you sure had me going," said Tiller, his tail starting to wag. "I thought I was a goner."

"You almost were," said Turnbuckle. "Remember Gunwale the Gator. He's not one of the parrot pirates."

"You mean he really would have…"

"Correct, my friend," said Mizzen. "It would have been over in one big bite."

"Sorry, Tiller," said Turnbuckle. "We didn't plan on you getting lost. That's why I sent Stem and Stern to warn you."

"And dis Caribbean parrot did not tink you would escape," said Pearl.

"I wouldn't have escaped if it hadn't been for Rachel Lanier and the flame," replied Tiller.

"Dat flame gave you comfort and courage in d'dark, just the way it does for Rachel in d'grave," said Pearl. "But dat old flame, it just scare d'feathers off me."

"I could tell," said Tiller. "You flew out of that cemetery like a rocket."

Everyone laughed at a red faced Pearl, but Tiller tried to make him feel better. "That's okay Pearl. I thought it was awfully nice of you to send the beautiful lady with the lantern to show me the way to the fort."

The parrot pirates all looked at each other. "Pearl didn't send her," said Turnbuckle. "Was this lady dressed in white, riding a white horse, and carrying a lantern?"

"Yes."

"That was a real ghost. Her name is Mary the Wanderer," said Turnbuckle. "Were you scared?"

"Of course not. What could be scary on this island?"

"Well, matey, for being so close to death and for being such a good sport," said Skipper the Sparrow, "we are making you an honorary member of the Parrot Pirate Gang."

Black Beak hoisted a Parrot Pirate pennant up the mast of Dogspeed while Keel raised the newly repaired mainsail. Stem and Stern saluted with their wings.

"Wow, I don't know how to thank you guys," said Tiller.

"I have an idea," said Mizzen. "How about treating the gang to dinner at our favorite hangout? It's just off the island in the town of Brunswick."

"That sounds like a great idea. What's the name of this place?" asked Tiller.

The gang just looked around at each other and smiled. Finally, Skipper the Sparrow said, "We'll keep that a surprise until we get there."

Tiller replied, "Boy, you guys are full of surprises."

"Just stick with us, sailor. You haven't seen anything yet!" promised Mizzen.

"So, can we sail to this hangout?" asked Tiller.

"Sure can," replied the Skipper, "and this is the perfect moonlit night for a sail."

"Then hop aboard, mateys, the Parrot Pirate Gang is sailing off to dinner," said Tiller.

With the light of the moon to guide them, they enjoyed a leisurely sail to Brunswick. There was much laughter and storytelling, and they all became good friends. Tiller thought he saw an alligator swimming as fast as it could for Jekyll Island. Dogspeed sailed well with her newly repaired sail, and the Parrot Pirate Gang took turns steering. When it was Stern's turn, he got off course and ran the boat aground in shallow water. They weren't stuck in the mud for very long because all the parrots, and the seagulls, grabbed the railing of Dogspeed and flew straight up in the air at the same time. The boat lifted right off the bottom, and they sailed merrily on their way.

Once in Brunswick, Dogspeed was tied securely to the dock and everyone jumped ashore. "Now," said Pearl, "we are goin' to put d'hood back over your head for d'trip to d'hangout."

"Not again!" said Tiller.

"Don't worry," said Turnbuckle, "we just want to see the look on your face when we take off the hood and you see the hangout for the first time."

"I can't wait," said Tiller. "This must be some special place."

"Let's just say that your wiener tail will be waggin'," replied Baggiewrinkle.

After a bumpy ride on the back of a truck from the local paper mill, the gang arrived at the hangout and stood in front of Tiller where they could see his face. Alee pulled the hood off Tiller's head while the whole gang said, "Ta Da!"

Tiller stood looking in amazement at a large sign hanging in front of a small restaurant that read:

HOT DOGS

"We Relish Your Bun"

WILLIE'S WEE-NEE WAGON

He laughed so hard that his sides began to hurt. The whole gang laughed with him until they were all rolling around in the parking lot.

Once they had regained most of their composure, Alee said, "Willie's Wee-Nee Wagon is a landmark here in Brunswick. No wiener can leave without having a weenie! What do you say, dog?"

"The dogs are on me," said Tiller, heading for the front door.

After a delicious dinner of dogs, the whole gang, stuffed and barely able to walk, or fly, gathered in the parking lot of Willie's to say goodbye. During dinner, Tiller and Turnbuckle had told the gang about their plans to sail the ocean blue.

"We sure will miss you both," said Skipper the Sparrow.

"Y'all come back now, ya hear?" said Keel.

Tiller and Turnbuckle smiled at each other, for they already knew they would return often. "We will," said Tiller and Turnbuckle at the same time.

"Besides," said Turnbuckle, "I doubt we'll get dogs this great on the Chesapeake."

Tiller smiled proudly at Turnbuckle, for she had pronounced "Chesapeake" perfectly for the first time.

After many hugs, the gang went their own way. Of course, Stem flew north and Stern flew south. Tiller, Turnbuckle, Baggiewrinkle, and Alee sailed Dogspeed back to East Beach on St. Simons Island. The light from the moon cast a silver glow on the water as they anchored the boat and doggie and cat paddled ashore. It was low tide, so they decided to walk home along the moonlit beach. They talked and laughed and skipped the whole way.

"Mom will be asleep. Let's tiptoe onto the screened-in porch and just sleep on the floor," suggested Turnbuckle. After all the excitement of the day, it didn't take long before they were fast asleep.

Chapter Thirteen

Waving Goodbye

As the first light of day crept onto the porch, Tiller stretched his paws, sat up, and looked over at Turnbuckle who was already awake. "Good morning, Turnbuckle," he said. "Have you been awake long?"

"I have for a little while. I can't sleep once the sun starts coming up, and I just love chasing the fiddler crabs off the porch early in the morning. It's also my favorite time of day to sit and talk with my mom. We talk every morning. I'm sure going to miss that, and I know she will, too."

"Where are Baggiewrinkle and Alee?" asked Tiller.

"They were playing with a fiddler on the roof. I think they chased it back down to the rocks."

"Why don't you go talk to your mom, and I'll play with Baggiewrinkle and Alee."

"Thanks, Tiller."

Turnbuckle walked into the kitchen and her mom was already sitting at the table. "Morning, Mom," she said.

"Good morning, dear." Mom had Turnbuckle's favorite morning treat ready for her. "I warmed up your milk just the way you like it."

"Thanks," replied Turnbuckle. "Mom, Tiller asked me to go with him on some sailing adventures, but I've never been away from home before. I know I don't scare easily, but I'm scared. Besides, who's going to warm my milk just the way I like it?"

"Turnbuckle, it's been your dream to have adventures beyond the world of St. Simons. All cats leave home sooner or later, for that is the way we cats are. I want you to live your dream and know that Baggiewinkle, Alee, and I love you very much. And there will be plenty of warm milk for you when you come back to visit."

"Thanks, Mom. I feel much better."

Turnbuckle licked her warm milk while she and her mom talked cat girl talk.

"I'd better go rescue Tiller from the little devils," said Turnbuckle when she finished her milk.

She gave her mom a big hug and ran to the porch. Tiller, Baggiewrinkle, and Alee were laughing and rolling in the sand down by the water. They looked like a hairy brown and calico ball with paws and tails sticking out. "Hey you three, its time for tea on the porch," called Turnbuckle. She stood aside in the doorway as the three charged past her.

While they all sat waiting for their sweet tea, Turnbuckle told Baggiewrinkle and Alee about her conversation with their mom.

"We have some advice for you, Turnbuckle," said Alee. "Always remember what 'grits' stands for."

"I know–girls raised in the south," said Turnbuckle with a giggle.

"And don't forget your sense of humor," said Baggiewrinkle. "I guess I'll be the one playing the tricks around here now." He looked at Alee with a mischievous smile.

"Well, Turnbuckle, are you ready for your first sailing adventure?" asked Tiller.

"You bet I am!"

Just then, Mom walked onto the porch with sweet tea for everyone. She also brought two lunches and plenty of sweet tea for Tiller and Turnbuckle's trip back to the Chesapeake Bay.

They sat in the shade of the porch talking and laughing. The cool morning air gave way to the sun's warm afternoon rays, and Tiller sensed that it was time to go. "Now that I've relaxed, sipped tea, and laughed a bunch on the porch, I feel as though I am officially a southerner," said Tiller.

"And you are officially part of the family, too," said Mom as she gave Tiller a big hug. "You two be careful."

"We will," they replied. After more hugs, Tiller and Turnbuckle gathered up their goodies to leave, but as she and Tiller headed for the door, Turnbuckle remembered a story that she and her mom used to read together called *Love You Forever*. There was something special from that story that she always said to her mom. This was just the right moment to say it.

"I'll love you forever.
I'll like you for always.
As long as I'm living,
My mommy you'll be."

With their eyes a little misty, Turnbuckle and her mom hugged one more time.

As Tiller and Turnbuckle slowly set off down the beach, they looked back and waved to Mom, Baggiewrinkle, and Alee, who were standing on the screened-in porch. Two seagulls were asleep on the roof. One was facing the beach and one was facing the road.

Turnbuckle said," Boy, this leaving home thing is harder than I thought."

"Don't think of it as leaving home. We'll be back. We'll always come back to St. Simons Island," said Tiller.

Turnbuckle smiled at Tiller. Mom, Baggiewrinkle, and Alee smiled as they waved, for they knew that Tiller and Turnbuckle would return to the island.

Tiller and Turnbuckle slowly sailed away from St. Simons Island. They waved goodbye to the white sand dunes of East Beach and to the tall lighthouse and to a large gray pelican sitting on a sea buoy. Then they sailed and sailed and sailed until they found themselves sailing the ocean blue.

"As long as the wind blows, we're going to keep sailing," said Tiller and Turnbuckle to the birds and the sky and the fish and the water.

"Wow! I loved that story, Grandpa," said Dinghy.

"Me too!" said Luff and Boom and Rudder and Starboard and Cleat and Anchor at the same time.

Grandpa smiled with delight, because, more than anything, he enjoyed telling a goodnight story to his seven grand puppies.

"Grandpa, are you friends with Tiller and Turnbuckle?" asked a curious Cleat.

"Yes, Cleat. You might say that," said Grandpa with a twinkle in his eye.

"How do you know them?" asked Anchor.

"Maybe I'll save that for next time," answered Grandpa.

"*Tell us another Tiller and Turnbuckle adventure right now, Grandpa,*" *the puppies pleaded.*

"*If you promise to go right to bed,*" *said Grandpa in a gentle Grandpa Dachshund sort of way,* "*I will tell you another one tomorrow night.*"

The seven puppies yelped for joy and snuggled back together again in a great furry ball...except for Dinghy who ran off to the tree one more time.

"*Oh Dinghy, not again,*" *said Rudder.*

Dinghy scampered back into the pile. "*Ouch, that hurt. This time you landed on my stomach,*" *said Boom.*

"*Sorry! Okay Grandpa, you can turn out the lights now,*" *said Dinghy.*

"*Pleasant dreams, precious puppies,*" *said Grandpa softly as he turned out the light.*

That night, seven little puppies all had sweet dreams of sailing the ocean blue.

A Glossary of Salty Words

Alee (uh lee)
on the leeward side or the side away from the wind

Anchor (ang ker)
a hook-like device dropped by chain or rope to keep a boat in one place

Baggiewrinkle (bag ee rink l)
clumps of frayed rope that protect the sails from rubbing against the lines

Boom (boom)
a pole extending from the mast that is attached to the bottom of the sail

Buoy (boo ee)
a floating device that marks a deep water channel or a hazard

Cleat (kleet)
a strip of metal or wood with arms on each end that a rope is tied around, usually to hold a boat against a dock

Dinghy (ding ee)
a small boat used to carry people and supplies to and
from a larger boat

Gull (guhl)
short for seagull

Gunwale (gun l)
the rail around the edge of a boat

Hatch (hach)
a door or opening in the deck of a boat

Keel (keel)
a flat surface on the bottom of a boat that keeps the
boat from slipping sideways; its weight also helps to keep
the boat upright

Luff (luhf)
when the sails shake as a boat is steered directly into the
wind; also, the front edge of a sail

Mainsail (meyn suhl)
a sail attached to the mainmast, usually in the middle
of a boat

Mizzen (miz uhn)
a small sail near the back of a boat

Poop deck (poop deck)
a deck on the back of a boat, usually raised to make it easier to see while steering

Porthole (pohrt hohl)
a window, usually round, in the side of a boat that can be opened and closed

Rudder (ruhd er)
a flat surface attached to the back of a boat used for steering

Seaworthy (see wur thee)
strong enough or fit enough for a voyage at sea

Skipper (skip er)
a nickname for the captain of a boat

Sloop (sloop)
a sailboat having only one mast with a mainsail and one sail in front of the mast called a foresail

Starboard (star berd)
the side of a boat that is on the right when a person faces forward

Stem (stem)
the forward edge of the bow

Stern (sturn)
the back or aft part of a boat

Tiller (til er)
a pole, usually wood, attached to the top of the rudder
to steer a small boat

Turnbuckle (turn buhk uhl)
a metal fitting that can be turned to tighten or loosen a
rope or wire, called a stay, that holds the mast in place